W9-DGH-416

Check out what RT Book Reviews *is saying about Rhonda Nelson's heroes in—and out of—uniform!*

Letters from Home
"This highly romantic tale is filled with emotion and wonderful characters. It's a heart-melting romance."

The Soldier
"Wonderfully written and heart-stirring, the story flies by to the deeply satisfying ending."

The Hell-Raiser
"A highly entertaining story that has eccentric secondary characters, hot sex and a heartwarming romance."

The Loner
"A highly romantic story with two heartwarming characters and a surprise ending.

The Ranger
"Well plotted and wickedly sexy, this one's got it all—including a completely scrumptious hero. A keeper."

Dear Reader,

Thank you so much for picking up *The Wild Card*. I never tire of writing these sinfully wicked, but oh-so-honorable Men Out of Uniform. These guys are all Southern gentlemen—so they know how to treat a lady and they're always quick-witted, fearless and lethally charming. An excellent combination, wouldn't you say?

Having made a deathbed promise to his mother to leave the military as soon as his next tour was up, Seth McCutcheon has no intention of going back on his word. He'd promised. He would deliver. Seth has absolutely no idea what he's going to do once he leaves though, and is both relieved and honored when Colonel Carl Garrett makes a recommendation on his behalf to Ranger Security.

But when Seth is tapped to provide security at a high-profile wedding, he soon begins to think that he preferred dodging bullets to dodging angry brides. And the wedding planner he has to pretend to be in love with? Make believe has never been more fun.

Nothing brings a smile to my face faster than hearing from my readers, so be sure to check out my website at www.ReadRhondaNelson.com.

Happy reading!

Rhonda Nelson

Rhonda Nelson

THE WILD CARD

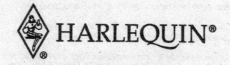

TORONTO • NEW YORK • LONDON
AMSTERDAM • PARIS • SYDNEY • HAMBURG
STOCKHOLM • ATHENS • TOKYO • MILAN • MADRID
PRAGUE • WARSAW • BUDAPEST • AUCKLAND

If you purchased this book without a cover you should be aware that this book is stolen property. It was reported as "unsold and destroyed" to the publisher, and neither the author nor the publisher has received any payment for this "stripped book."

Recycling programs
for this product may
not exist in your area.

ISBN-13: 978-0-373-79598-7

THE WILD CARD

Copyright © 2011 by Rhonda Nelson

All rights reserved. Except for use in any review, the reproduction or utilization of this work in whole or in part in any form by any electronic, mechanical or other means, now known or hereafter invented, including xerography, photocopying and recording, or in any information storage or retrieval system, is forbidden without the written permission of the publisher, Harlequin Enterprises Limited, 225 Duncan Mill Road, Don Mills, Ontario M3B 3K9, Canada.

This is a work of fiction. Names, characters, places and incidents are either the product of the author's imagination or are used fictitiously, and any resemblance to actual persons, living or dead, business establishments, events or locales is entirely coincidental.

This edition published by arrangement with Harlequin Books S.A.

For questions and comments about the quality of this book please contact us at Customer_eCare@Harlequin.ca.

® and TM are trademarks of the publisher. Trademarks indicated with ® are registered in the United States Patent and Trademark Office, the Canadian Trade Marks Office and in other countries.

www.eHarlequin.com

Printed in U.S.A.

ABOUT THE AUTHOR

A Waldenbooks bestselling author, two-time RITA® Award nominee and *RT Book Reviews* Reviewers' Choice nominee, Rhonda Nelson writes hot romantic comedy for the Harlequin Blaze line and other Harlequin imprints. With more than twenty-five published books to her credit and many more coming down the pike, she's thrilled with her career and enjoys dreaming up her characters and manipulating the worlds they live in. In addition to a writing career, she has a husband, two adorable kids, a black Lab and a beautiful bichon frise. She and her family make their chaotic but happy home in a small town in northern Alabama. She loves to hear from her readers, so be sure and check her out at www.ReadRhondaNelson.com.

Books by Rhonda Nelson

HARLEQUIN BLAZE

Don't miss any of our special offers. Write to us at the following address for information on our newest releases.

Harlequin Reader Service
U.S.: 3010 Walden Ave., P.O. Box 1325, Buffalo, NY 14269
Canadian: P.O. Box 609, Fort Erie, Ont. L2A 5X3

For my brother,
whose character and wit is in every hero I write.

1

As an active Ranger in Uncle Sam's service who had performed more tours of duty than he could remember, Seth McCutcheon was used to seeing terrible things. But watching his mother die was definitely the worst.

"Mom, you need to rest," he chided softly, his throat thick. Lamplight glowed against the side of her face, illuminating her smooth cheeks, the faint laugh lines around her eyes. She was fifty-two. Too young to be at the end of her life, a vibrant one that had been spent making sure that he and his little sister had been provided for. His gaze slid to the vase of daisies on her nightstand, her "happy" flowers, and his lips twitched in a weary smile.

"Tired of losing to me, are you?" his mother asked, a weak laugh shaking her unbelievably frail shoulders. She looked up from the cards in her hand and eyed him shrewdly. "You're not letting me win, are you?"

Under the circumstances he would have, but it hadn't been necessary. She'd always been able to beat him at poker, one of the few people who had, if he was quite honest. She'd taught him, after all. It only seemed fitting.

"You know damned well I'm not letting you win," he told her, rolling his shoulders against the ache that had settled there. He'd been sitting at her bedside for hours, afraid to leave, afraid to miss a single second with her in case the next might be her last. "You're trouncing me," he complained good-naturedly. "If I were letting you win, I'd at least put on a good enough show that you wouldn't know it."

She hummed under her breath, consulting her cards. "True enough, I suppose, but I do wish you'd make more of an effort, Seth. I'm about to up the ante in a way that's going to seriously impact your future. You'd do well to get your head in the game." Her tone was deceptively light, but he knew better.

Seth stilled and looked up. "Up the ante? What are you talking about?"

She smiled wearily. "I have little use for money," she said. "Soon enough I'm not going to need it. I—"

"Mom," he interrupted, panic and dread making his heart race.

She set her cards aside, then reached over and took his hand. Her bright blue eyes were soft and full of compassion. Comforting *him*, when it should have been the other way around. *Jeez God, how was he going to get through this?*

"Seth, I know that you don't want to have this conversation, but it's one that has to take place. There are things we have to talk about before I shuffle off this mortal coil," she said in an attempt to season the terrible conversation with humor. "You know that. Please just listen."

She was right. He didn't want to have the conversation, he'd never imagined that they'd be having it so soon. They'd only found the cancer four months ago—in her brain, no less. She'd undergone high doses of chemotherapy, causing her to lose more than twenty pounds and all of her hair. She currently wore an outrageous long blond wig, one that put him in mind of a Barbie doll. He'd been shocked when he'd first seen her in it—the first of many—but she'd merely laughed and said that the good Lord hadn't blessed her with long hair of any sort and that this provided the perfect opportunity to try out different styles. Her glass was firmly half-full, even in the midst of this horrible disease. Seth looked heavenward and gave a grunt, his chest feeling as if it were locked in Satan's vise grip.

Only his mother.

His eyes burned, but he tried for a smile all the same and gave her hand a squeeze. She was right. They couldn't put it off much longer. She was getting weaker every day—in part, he was sure, because she refused to sleep more than a couple of hours at a time. She'd even made both him and his sister promise to wake her. She didn't want to waste whatever time she had left by sleeping, she'd said. Were their positions reversed, Seth knew he'd likely feel the same way. Still…

He finally nodded, silently encouraging her to go on.

"Let's get the grisly part over first, shall we? I don't want a traditional funeral."

He snorted before he could stop himself.

She laughed. "Yes, yes, I know. I'm predictably un-predictable, but I don't care. The idea of all my friends and family gawking over my dead body lying in a cof-fin, talking about how 'good' I look while I'm *dead,* for pity's sake, is just more than I can bear. Cremate me and scatter my ashes among my roses, where I'll do some good."

So that she'd still be useful…and still here. How was he going to get through this? he wondered again. How was the world going to go on when she was no longer a part of it? She'd always been there for him. Bandaging scraped knees, nursing colds, tossing the football with him in the backyard. A constant source of love and encouragement, one he'd realized too late he'd taken for granted.

"My will is in the desk over there," she said, jerking her head in that direction. She picked up her cards once more. "It's simple enough. I don't have much, but what I have is yours and your sister's." She paused. "I want Katie to have the house. Since Rat Bastard left she's been having a hard time making ends meet and I don't want that for her and Mitchell."

Seth was in full agreement there. "Rat Bastard's" real name was actually Michael, and he'd recently left Seth's sister and child and moved in with the girl who worked as the jelly doughnut filler at the local pastry shop. When the time was right, Seth fully intended to pay a visit to Michael and give him a lesson in how to treat a lady, most specifically, his sister.

He'd already given that same lesson to his father, the faithless, miserable, weak-willed son of a bitch.

"I've had the house appraised," his mother continued. "And I've made provisions in the will to offset what your part would have been if I hadn't left the house to Katie."

"Mom, you didn't have to do that. She can have it all. I don't want—"

"Fair is fair," she insisted. "I've been paying those life insurance premiums all these years just in case something happened and it's a comfort for me to know that your sister will have this house and you'll have a little money to put toward your own."

Because he didn't want to upset her, he didn't point out the obvious. Seth didn't need a "home." His home was in the military.

She smiled weakly. "I know what you're thinking, son, and that's where my ante comes in. When I'm gone, your sister and Mitchell aren't going to have anyone—" She swallowed, betraying the first crack in her resolve. That single fissure absolutely shattered him. "And I'd feel a whole lot better if I knew that you'd be coming home when your contract runs out."

"Mom," he said, shaking his head. *Not this, anything but this.* "You know—"

"I *do* know, Seth," she interrupted. "I know that you love your job, that the military has been your life. I do know," she repeated softly. "It pains me to ask and hurts even more that I have to." She swallowed again. "But I also know that if something happened to you, Katie and Mitchell would be completely, utterly alone...and I just can't bear that. And neither could they."

It was a terribly bleak picture, but one that was equally accurate, should the worst happen. He thought of his sister, hardworking and funny. His nephew, only two years old, with curly blond hair and big brown eyes.

"Play me for it," his mother said, glancing shrewdly at him above her cards. "If I win this hand, then you come out as soon as you can. If you win, then you do whatever you feel is right."

A bark of laughter erupted from his thickening throat and he watched her lips twist. "Meaning if I don't come out, then I'm a selfish, uncaring bastard." He shook his head. "Excellent. Great choices there."

His mother chuckled. "I'm being shamelessly manipulative, I know, but..."

He looked up at her. "And you're also holding a winning hand, otherwise you wouldn't have brought it up now."

His mother merely stared at him, betraying nothing. "Are you in or out?"

Seth consulted his own cards. He was pretty confident, not that it would matter. He'd already lost. "In," he said.

"Let's see what you've got," his mother said.

Seth laid his hand down. "Three of a kind, kings high."

His mother quirked a brow. "You and those wild cards," she *tsked,* noticing the one in his hand. "Those one-eyed jacks always find their way to you, don't they?"

Yeah, they did. He'd actually been given the nickname the Wild Card when he'd been in Jump School, and had a tattoo of one on his right shoulder to commemorate the moniker. Of course, considering that Seth's methods were occasionally deemed unorthodox at best and reckless at worst, the name served double duty.

He merely shrugged, smiling. "They do seem to favor me."

His mother's lips lifted in a grin that made a sick feeling in his belly take hold. She laid down her cards. "They favored me with this hand, too," she said, sliding a finger over the edge of the jack of hearts.

Four of a kind, aces high.

Shit.

His lips twisted. "Well played, Mom," he said, mentally watching his future roll out in a direction he had never anticipated, never wanted.

She arched an eyebrow, but the relief in her face was so stark it was painful. "I have your word?"

He nodded, struggling to speak. "Of course."

Seemingly satisfied that she'd completed an important task on her last to-do list, every muscle in her body relaxed and she settled more firmly into her bed. "Good," she said, her voice thin. "Thank you. You're a good man, Seth. My sweet boy," she murmured. Her eyes drifted over his face with affection—a look he'd seen hundreds of times—then fluttered shut.

"You should rest," he chided, his eyes stinging. "I'm tiring you out."

She laced her fingers through his. "I do think I'll take

a little nap. Wake me in two hours," she said, giving his hand a firm squeeze. "Don't forget."

"I won't, Mom."

Exactly one-hundred-and-twenty minutes later, he tried...but didn't succeed.

2

Seven months later...

"PAYNE HAS impeccable taste and Jamie lets his better half dress him, but no one—not even his lovely wife, evidently—can convince Guy McCann that camouflage isn't proper wedding attire," the slim man behind the desk was saying when Seth approached. The office manager, he presumed, held up one finger, indicating that he would only be a moment longer, and shot Seth an apologetic look. The man's gaze dropped down to a photo on his frighteningly immaculate desk and he gave a delicate shudder. "Yes, Terrence, yes. He's wearing *camo pants* and a *black t-shirt*. That's what the cretin wore to the wedding. Tanner gave me a photo this morning. I'm looking at it right now." He exhaled mightily again, as though the camo-wearer's sin against fashion was almost more than he could bear. Seth couldn't quite reconcile this outraged put-upon Latino as an employee of Ranger Security. "You're right, of course, but camo?

At a wedding? Yes, yes. All right. I'll see you later, then."

The man uttered a swift goodbye, then disconnected. His quick gaze snapped up to Seth's. "Sorry about that," he said, his tone immediately professional. "I don't ordinarily take personal phone calls on the job, but in this case I made an exception. You're Seth McCutcheon, correct?"

Seth nodded, making an effort to flatten his twitching lips.

"I'm Juan-Carlos, the office manager here at Ranger Security." He selected a file from the corner of his desk and gestured for Seth to follow him. "Come with me, please. They're waiting for you in the boardroom." The last sentence was delivered with a curiously sarcastic bent.

And thirty seconds later, Seth understood why.

The boardroom, as it were, didn't have the traditional table and rolling executive chairs. Instead, it more resembled a high-tech clubhouse, complete with a pool table, a huge, flat-panel television anchored to the wall and lots of comfortable leather furniture. A stainless steel side-by-side refrigerator stood in the kitchenette and a host of different snacks were lined up in old-fashioned candy jars along the counter. Everything from biscotti to Pixy Stix—his childhood favorite—were represented, bringing a smile to his lips.

Jamie Flanagan and Guy McCann—he recognized them from the research he'd done—were playing a war game on the Xbox and Brian Payne sat in a recliner, perusing a file. He looked up when Juan-Carlos announced Seth and immediately stood.

"Seth," he said, extending his hand. "Brian Payne. It's good to have you here."

McCann and Flanagan immediately put their game on hold, setting their controllers aside to welcome him. Juan-Carlos heaved a long-suffering, but seemingly resigned, sigh as he looked at McCann. Then, with a tragic baffled shake of his head, he left the room.

As soon as the door shut behind Juan-Carlos, Flanagan and McCann broke into gut-clenching guffaws, while Payne merely chuckled.

"Sorry," Payne told him. "McCann has been playing with Photoshop and has been torturing our long-suffering but *irreplaceable* office manager," he said, shooting the other two a dark look.

Ah. Seth inclined his head and smiled, looking at McCann. "So you didn't really wear camo to a wedding?"

Still wheezing with laughter, McCann shook his head. "No, but it's been *huge* fun letting Juan-Carlos think I did."

"I can't believe he fell for it," Jamie remarked. "I mean, I know you're a not a fashion icon—" he glanced meaningfully at the jeans and Alabama T-shirt Guy currently wore "—but the guy should know that even *you* have some sense of propriety."

Still laughing, Guy looked up. "Did he show you the picture?"

Seth shook his head. "No, but he was talking about it to someone on the phone when I came in."

"Sweet," McCann crowed, looking jubilant. "A colleague of ours—and now yours—Tanner Crawford, married in Asheville a while back and the three of us made the drive over to celebrate the nuptials with the happy couple," McCann explained. "Juan-Carlos had been invited, as well—"

"Because he gets pissed off if he isn't included," Jamie interjected.

"—but he'd had tickets to an Elton John concert and didn't want to miss it." McCann grinned. "For kicks, I've been playing around with the wedding photos just to needle him," he said. "It's provided hours of entertainment."

So they were practical jokers? Seth thought, feeling more at ease. He and his friends had been notorious for that, as well. He'd once had an entire eyebrow shaved off after a night of too much alcohol and too little sleep. It had taken much longer than he'd ever imagined to grow it back.

"Would you like something to drink?" Payne offered. "Coffee? Tea? A soda?"

Seth shook his head. "I'm good, thanks."

Flanagan gestured for him to take a seat and they all settled in. The atmosphere was relaxed and warm. The camaraderie between the three men was enviable. These guys weren't just comfortable in their own skins, they were comfortable with each other.

That was one of the things that he'd most hated about leaving the military, Seth thought. Aside from it being his purpose, his way of life, his best friends were there. Finn O'Conner—who had recently become engaged to his childhood sweetheart and planned to move to Tybee Island to run an old motor inn when he came out—and Greer West had been part of his crew since ROTC. And, though he knew they both understood why he'd had to get out, he couldn't help but feel he'd betrayed a trust of sorts. As if his defection had broken something that might not ever be completely repaired. Or maybe that was simply the guilt talking. He felt he'd abandoned them. And leaving the service during a time of war…

That was the worst. Knowing that his country needed him, that his fellow soldiers needed him. And he was here, about to take a cushy job protecting politicians, debutantes, celebrities and people with more money than sense. Where was the honor in that? And better still, how did these guys find it?

"You've reviewed the employment offer?" Payne asked.

Seth nodded. To say that it was generous would be a vast understatement. In addition to the extremely healthy salary, he'd been given an apartment, as well. He had to admit that was a perk he sincerely appreciated. As much as he loved Katie and Mitchell, living with them was another matter altogether. Katie was under the semi-accurate impression that she and Mitch would cramp his dating style. While that was a legitimate concern, it wasn't his primary reason for wanting his own space. He'd given up his career to come back here and be there for them—he didn't think having a little privacy was too much to ask. Besides, being in that house without his mother felt…wrong. He hoped someday it would be a comfort, but right now it was too much of a reminder of his loss.

"Do you have any questions? Any concerns?" Payne asked.

None that he could go into without insulting them, Seth thought. Colonel Carl Garrett had recommended him for this job and, ultimately, he was eternally thankful to have it. He'd be working with former Rangers, men he understood, doing a job he was overqualified for, but equally overpaid. It wasn't their place to make him feel this new direction his life had taken had purpose—that was his own to sort out. Obviously these men had walked the same path—under different, more tragic circumstances, he knew—and they'd found their way.

He would find his. Hopefully sooner rather than later.

And he couldn't find it with better men.

Known in certain circles as the Specialist, Brian Payne was coolly efficient and had strategy down to an art form. With an unmatched attention to detail, there was no such thing as half-assed in his world. He didn't tolerate it.

Jamie Flanagan purportedly sported a genius-level IQ and had been the original player until he met and married Colonel Garrett's granddaughter. That quick brain, combined with a substantial amount of brawn, made him a force to be reckoned with.

And with a lucky streak that bordered on the divine, Guy McCann's ability to skate the thin line between recklessness and perfection was still locker-room lore.

Much like his, Guy's methods were governed more

by his gut than his head and, thus far, his gut hadn't failed him. Had Seth been orchestrating the prank on Juan-Carlos, he would have put the groom in camo, the bride in a Hooter's T-shirt and the pastor in a wife-beater undershirt. He inwardly smiled, wishing he knew them well enough at this point to say so. It would come, he knew, but building those kinds of relationships took time, something he certainly had plenty of now. He mentally grimaced.

Payne and the other two shared a look and Seth got the distinct impression that an entire unspoken conversation had passed between them.

That kind of communication took time, too.

"Listen, Seth," Payne said. "Ordinarily when the Colonel sends us new recruits, we know those guys are getting out because they want to. They've reached a point in their careers where, for whatever reason, they're no longer able or willing to do the job." He paused. "As we understand it, you were not at that point."

To be less than honest wouldn't be fair, but that didn't make him any more eager to have this discussion. Nevertheless, like so many others recently, it was a conversation he would have to have. He swallowed a sigh.

"No, I was not," Seth admitted. "I'd intended to make a full career of the military. It's what I'd envisioned when I went in and an alternate path—or occupation, for that matter—was never in any future I'd planned."

"You were ROTC, right?" Jamie asked. "Through the University of Georgia?"

Seth nodded. Go Dogs. He was still a huge fan and

proud alumnus. Judging from the Alabama memorabilia scattered about the room, so were they. Nick Saban had secured the Tide's thirteenth National Championship, but the perpetually unsmiling coach still had a long way to go before he could ever reach Bear Bryant's legendary status, if you asked him.

Seth released a slow breath, hoping to ease some of the sudden tension from his chest. "But, as I'm sure the colonel told you, I lost my mother seven months ago and I promised her that I would come out as soon as I could. I've got a little sister and a nephew and, without getting into too much family history—" he'd just as soon boil his balls in acid, thank you very much "—I'm the only family they have." And vice versa, of course, he suddenly realized, the thought giving him an odd pause. He blinked, struggling to focus. "She wanted me to be around for them," he finally managed to say. "I made a promise, so I'm here."

"Well, it goes without saying that we're glad you are," Payne said. "We know this will be an adjustment for you, but have every confidence that you'll be up for whatever we throw at you."

"And I am particularly glad you're here," McCann chimed in with a chuckle, popping the top on an energy drink. "Because that means you're going to take my place on Ono Island this weekend." He scratched his chin in apparent bafflement. "Curiously, Julia doesn't like it when I pretend to be in love with another woman."

If he'd been eating something he would have choked. "I'm sorry?"

Before he could recover, Payne opened the file he'd been reading when he came in. He sent a cool stare in Guy's direction, but Guy merely bit the end off a piece of red licorice and grinned unrepentantly.

"Trent McWilliams," Payne said, arching a blond eyebrow. "Does the name ring a bell?"

Seth's jaw nearly unhinged. "As in the quarterback for the Orlando Mustangs? *That* Trent McWilliams?" He was South eastern Conference royalty, was a first-round draft pick and a born-and-bred Alabama boy. He was supposedly good-looking—he'd have to be when one considered he had an entire fan base who'd nicknamed themselves "Trent's Tarts" and hung out with country music superstars and the Hollywood elite. He wasn't just a mega-talented quarterback, he was a star in his own right.

Payne flashed a smile. "That would be the one. Trent's been having some security issues, issues that seem to be escalating the closer it gets to his wedding date, which is this weekend. We've been running point for him for the past several weeks trying to isolate the threat." He grimaced. "So far we haven't had any luck."

Seth found himself more intrigued than he'd expected. He savored the adrenaline that shot into his system. "What sort of threats?"

"Well, you've always got the run-of-the-mill overzealous fans," Jamie drawled, leaning forward. "The ones who have watched all the games, every bit of YouTube footage, have read every interview and believe that they have a *unique* connection to the object of their misplaced attention. You've got the obsessive letter writer who critiques every game and sends his notes and suggestions, the toenail-clipping woman, who mailed her 'collection' as a gift."

They all grimaced.

"Then there's the women," Guy chimed in. "The constant propositioning, the barrage of nude photos."

"And then there's stuff like this," Payne said, his tone subdued, handing Seth a sheet of paper that had been slipped into a page protector. "This was the first."

It was Trent McWilliams's wedding announcement, which had been printed from an online celebrity gossip site. The couple had been circled in red with a slash across the photo as though "banning" the couple. *Not no, but HELL no,* had been written in block-style capital letters across the bottom of the page.

"Initially, that one didn't raise too much concern," Payne told him. "It seemed harmless enough. Trent received dozens of letters from sad women denouncing the impending marriage. But when this one arrived a month later," he said, handing over another sheet, "*then* it became an issue."

Seth inspected the second paper. The same red pen, same barring symbol, but this one was over Trent and Nella's names. More significantly, on their save-the-date announcement. Which someone would have had to have received. Someone who wasn't a run-of-the-mill-psycho fan, but someone who was close…or too close for comfort at the very least. The hair on the back of Seth's neck prickled. *Call it off* was written in the block-style letters, again in red, on the bottom.

Now he understood.

"Ah," Seth murmured, studying the two. "How many people got a notice?"

"One hundred. They're hosting the wedding at Trent's place on Ono Island, so space is an issue. It's three acres max, with the house and guesthouse, various garages and the like. They're keeping it intimate, according to the wedding planner."

Guy snorted. "Intimate is *not* a hundred people. Intimate is five, with two of them being the bride and groom, and one being the preacher."

"Finally, Trent received this one two weeks ago." Payne handed over the last page.

It was the wedding invitation, which left no doubt that the threat was real. Whoever was sending the messages was relatively close to Trent. It was hand lettered, too, leaving no room to speculate that this was a copy. There was the banning symbol again, with *So it's to be death at a wedding, then? So be it,* printed in red along the bottom.

How bizarre, Seth thought. And ambiguous. Whose death? Trent's? His bride's? Or someone else's?

Better still, how was he supposed to protect every single one of the guests? One-hundred people plus the wedding party, not to mention the catering and service crews. Seth considered himself a pretty damned fine soldier, but he'd never quite mastered the handy ability to be everywhere at once. What, precisely, did they expect him to do? He could wing it, of course. He was certain that something would come to him—it always did—but he'd prefer to at least attempt to play by the rules on this first mission. He needed to establish their trust first, so that they wouldn't question him later when he did pull what his previous commanding officer liked to call his "stunts." Stunt or not, he always managed to get the job done.

"Naturally we don't expect you to protect every single person at the event," Payne told him, displaying the unsettling knack of plucking the thoughts right out of his head. "You're going to take over as point on security—"

"Disguised as the wedding planner's boyfriend," Guy interjected.

"—and, if you haven't isolated the threat by the rehearsal, then your purpose will shift to acting as personal bodyguard to Trent McWilliams and his intended bride."

In other words, if he wanted to avoid catastrophe, he needed to apprehend the culprit before someone died or ruined the wedding. Someone who had eluded these guys for several weeks.

Excellent.

Seth was considering his odds of actually keeping this job when something McCann said fully registered. "The wedding planner's boyfriend?" That sounded more ominous than he cared to contemplate. He didn't want to be anyone's boyfriend, pretend or otherwise. A friend with benefits was more to his liking, preferably one with an excellent sense of humor, a nice ass and her own address. Though Seth knew there were people who made the marriage and family plan work, he knew more people who didn't. While he wasn't opposed to taking risks, he nevertheless knew when to heed the odds.

Marriage, or any variation, wasn't for him.

He felt a nudge of dread prod his belly.

The wedding planner was probably going to have a sickeningly different attitude about it. Oh, jeez, he thought, becoming more alarmed by the second. She'd likely be a hopeless romantic bent on trying to convert him and anyone else who had the misguided audacity to want to remain single. No doubt his naked ring finger would be a challenge to her and she'd alternate between fits of perkiness and pity that would drive him insane.

Shit.

Perky women annoyed him. What the hell did they have to be so happy about anyway? he wondered, his mind quickly calculating how many levels of discomfort he'd have to endure over the course of this assignment. The seventh circle of hell sounded more appealing.

Granted, he had to admit it was a good idea—the wedding planner had access to everything and everyone involved on every level of the event. If he'd been pulling the plan together, he imagined this would have been his solution, too.

But for someone else. Not for *him.*

Payne handed him a photo. "Penelope Hart is the wedding planner. She's based here in Atlanta and was a sorority sister of the bride, Nella Francis."

"And she's—"

"—totally vetted," Payne supplied, anticipating his question.

Seth nodded, glad that they seemed to be thinking along the same lines, at any rate.

"Evidently Ms. Hart is the go-to girl for all fashionable

weddings in the area," Jamie said, his lips twisting with baffled humor. "I'd have married Audrey at a drive-through if she'd been game."

"That would have seriously wounded Juan-Carlos," Seth remarked, his gaze dropping to the image as the other three laughed.

A strange flutter moved through his belly as he looked at the woman in question. Curly black hair hung to her narrow shoulders and framed a face that was more startling than pretty. She had a wide forehead made softer with sleek, dark brows that winged over a pair of very bright blue eyes. Her skin had an olive tone that hinted of Italian origins and, though she was relatively fair in this photo, he could tell she was a girl who tanned easily. Her cheekbones rested high on her face, leaving sultry hollows beneath, and the mouth and chin that tied it altogether were simultaneously charming and sexy.

Pretty definitely didn't fit, Seth thought broodingly as he continued to study the photo. *Compelling* was a more apt description, he decided. She drew the eye and had the power to hold it. And, when it came right down to it, that was probably better than pretty. Pretty got boring.

She, he instinctively knew, would never be boring.

And the same instincts—these of the ball-tightening variety—that told him she wouldn't be boring also told him she'd be trouble.

He mentally swore. He didn't have time for trouble, pretty, interesting or otherwise.

"Penelope has been brought completely up to speed

and is fully willing to cooperate in any way possible," Payne told him.

He would imagine so, Seth thought. He didn't know a whole lot about the wedding planning industry, but he suspected that having a murder take place at one of the events she'd coordinated would be bad for business.

"You'll meet her tomorrow morning. Since parking is at a premium on the island and you're supposed to be a 'couple' anyway, you'll ride down with her. Will Forrester, Tanner Crawford and Lucas Finn will follow and the four of you will coordinate the security. As Ms. Hart's love interest, you'll be in closest proximity to Trent and Nella and, because of that, you'll run point."

That was certainly going to endear him to his fellow security specialists, Seth thought with an inward grimace. *Thanks, boys.* He appreciated *that* target on his back.

"You're also the only single guy here," Jamie told him. "And, as Guy pointed out earlier, women don't typically like it when their significant others pretend to be in love with other women."

Ah, Seth thought as understanding dawned. He didn't get point because of his untested skill—he'd gotten it because none of the rest of them wanted it. He didn't want it either, but as low man on the totem pole, he wasn't going to get a choice. He felt his lips twitch, reluctantly impressed with their plan. It was clever and devious, both traits he happened to admire.

A hint of humor lurked in Payne's cool gaze. "You're still unattached, correct?"

Seth nodded and smiled. And he had every intention of staying that way. Those weren't the kind of odds he liked to play with. What was the point, really? He'd never met a woman who made him want to do anything any different and he'd come to the conclusion that she didn't exist. "Quite happily, with no plans to change the status quo."

"Famous last words," Guy muttered with a significant eye roll.

Before Seth could form a rebuttal, Payne handed him a set of keys. "To your apartment," he told him. "You're on the third floor. It's furnished for now, but we can easily move those things out as you feather your nest, so to speak. Feel free to make any changes you want." Next he handed over a laptop case, a Glock 9 with a permit to carry concealed, a cell phone and the file for his first case. "You'll need to take a look at the file, then you're to meet the others this evening to go over strategy. We can't let anything get by on this one. This is as high profile as anything we've ever done and our reputation is fully on the line here."

No pressure, Seth thought.

"Five o'clock, your place okay?" Payne asked.

Even aware of the especially high stakes, Seth felt more confident with a plan in mind. He nodded. "Sounds good."

"I've told Ms. Hart to expect you at eight tomorrow morning. Her address is in the file. She's in Marietta."

The same as his sister and nephew, Seth thought. Familiar with the drive, he made a mental note to leave in plenty of time to compensate for the heavy morning traffic.

"You've got transportation?" Payne asked.

He did, a new-to-him quad-cab truck. It was midnight-blue with leather interior and a sunroof. When he'd pulled up in the big monster, his sister had merely smiled indulgently, shaken her head and asked if the tank he'd wanted hadn't been available. The smart-ass. Yes, it was big and yes, it wasn't exactly economically friendly, but he'd test driven other vehicles and decided that he'd rather be in something a little more substantial than a soup can. He recycled, dammit. It wasn't like he wasn't doing his part.

At his nod, Payne stood and extended his hand. "All right, then. Welcome aboard."

Seth got to his feet and his palm met Payne's. "Thank you. I appreciate the opportunity." He congratulated himself for the diplomatic response. He couldn't say that he was glad to be here, because that was a lie. He'd rather be with his guys, finishing the job they'd started. An image of his mother suddenly rose in his mind's eye and he swallowed.

But a promise was a promise.

And Seth McCutcheon was a man of his word.

PAYNE WAITED until their newest recruit was safely out of earshot before turning a questioning look at his friends and partners. "Well?"

"I like him," Guy said. "But it's obvious that he doesn't want to be here."

"Did any of us really want to be here to start with?"

Jamie asked. "Had Danny lived, would any of us be doing what we're doing? Or would we still be in the service?"

That was an excellent point, Payne thought. Had their good friend and unit mate Danny Levinson lived—had they not each felt responsible for his death in some way—would they have left the military? Would there even be a Ranger Security?

No, probably not.

But there also wouldn't be any wives and children, no one to go home to at the end of the day, no one to love… and that was a pretty damned miserable thought.

"I guess not," Guy said, suddenly somber. "But it's a damned shame that some sort of tragedy always brings new recruits to our door."

Because they didn't hire anyone without Colonel Carl Garrett's recommendation, as well as extensive background checks on their own, they knew as much as it was possible to know about Seth McCutcheon. So they'd been able to read a lot about his situation and his character simply by looking between the lines. His father had left when he was just five years old—old enough to remember him, but not to actually know him. Seth had been raised by his mother, a high school English teacher who supplemented her income by selling cosmetics on the side. By all accounts, she was highly regarded, deeply loved and, given that Seth had kept his promise to her after her death, even more respected.

Though he'd been voted Class Clown, he'd graduated valedictorian from his high school class, earned the ROTC scholarship, where he got a communications degree, then went through Jump School to complete his Ranger training.

Interviews with fellow soldiers painted the picture of a man very much like Guy, one who didn't always follow the play book, but never failed to get the desired result. He'd been nicknamed Wild Card and, though he'd only spent roughly thirty minutes in Seth's company, Payne could sense the same sort of irreverent energy in him he'd always associated with McCann. There was an intelligence and humor that lurked in his gaze that was unmistakably familiar.

In short, despite the fact that he didn't want to be here, that he'd never planned to leave the military, ultimately Payne thought Seth would eventually come to enjoy this career move. The work was different, certainly, but it was never boring and—his gaze slid to his friends—the company was first-rate.

As for this initial assignment… He chuckled.

Jamie glanced up. "What's so funny?"

"To make sure that our agent is up to speed on his role as her love interest, Penelope Hart sent a 'history' of them over today for Seth to review and learn before they make their debut on Ono Island."

A bark of laughter erupted from Guy's throat. "She did, did she?"

"Did you read it?" Jamie asked.

Payne nodded and released a slow breath. "Yep. And let's just say that if the wedding planning business ever fizzles out for her, then she's got an excellent future writing soap operas."

Guy grinned. "That good, eh?"

Payne lifted a bottle of soda to his lips. "Oh, yeah. I put it in the file."

"I'd like to be a fly on the wall when he reads it," Jamie remarked, chuckling under his breath.

He would, too, Payne thought. He would, too...

3

As A RULE, Penelope Hart didn't appreciate it when people showed up unexpectedly on her front doorstep, regardless of whether it was the Girl Scouts, the Jehovah's Witnesses, would-be politicians or cosmetic salesladies. She thought simply dropping by was rude and, though Southerners were famous for it, she still believed it was bad form to appear at another person's home, uninvited, unexpected and otherwise out of the blue.

That opinion was soon going to make her a giant hypocrite. Because she was about to do it herself.

Her would-be victim? The security specialist assigned to keep Trent and Nella safe. Why couldn't she wait until eight o'clock in the morning to meet him as scheduled? Her cheeks puffed as she exhaled mightily.

That was the million-dollar question.

On the drive over, Penelope had been telling herself that she needed to assess him herself, that she needed to make sure that, first, he was capable—as if Ranger Security hadn't already done that themselves she thought with a mental eye roll—and, second, he was believable boyfriend material for her.

If she was honest, that was the real reason she couldn't wait until the morning. She had to see him for herself—meet him for herself—if for no other reason than to make sure she could pull this off. All she knew about Seth McCutcheon was that he was a new hire and, as the only unattached man employed by the security company, he had to be *her* man.

Penelope understood that. Trying to pass him off as one of Trent's best friends or relatives wouldn't work due to the intimate nature of the wedding. The agency was plugging in three other security experts, as well. Each of those men would be going in disguised as service workers.

Since she was the wedding planner and would have access to every part of the event, having Seth working with her was a no-brainer. But putting him in as her boyfriend felt very…weird.

Especially since Penelope hadn't ever had a proper boyfriend.

Had she dated? Certainly. With regularity? Yes. But she never allowed things to progress past the fun stage, past the first blush of new romance. As such, the bloom was never fully off the rose. Meeting someone, that first sizzle of awareness, the prelude to that first kiss… that epitomized romance for her and that was all she was interested in. The minute she felt obligated to do anything—family functions, laundry, errands, what have you—for the guy she was dating, she instantly withdrew from the relationship and moved on to the next guy. She was never invested enough to care about the end of the relationship—translate: she never got hurt—and there were plenty of fish in the sea. Her lips quirked. Luckily, she was a pretty good angler.

As it happened, there was no next guy at the moment. So in that regard, pretending to have a boyfriend wasn't going to be a problem.

She'd be lying, though, if she didn't admit to a little bit of trepidation. Even pretending to be even semicommitted made her skin itch and her chest squeeze. Her friends often teased her about her chosen profession, considering that she never had any intention of getting married herself—her parents had *nine* marriages between the two of them, need she say more?—but it was *the* ultimate party and, when it came to planning, she was a pro. She always had been.

Her degree was actually in communications, but after hosting one party after another throughout college, then baby showers and the weddings of a few friends, she'd found her niche and had never looked back. Despite the fact that she never wanted to have a wedding herself, it was *the* grand event. Everything else—birthday parties, baby showers, etc.—was simply second tier.

Pen didn't do second tier.

Trent and Nella's wedding was her highest profile to date, and it went without saying that having this event go off without a hitch would fully cement her in her field. With that came financial security, something she'd been working toward since she was old enough to get a job. She'd grown up in a feast-or-famine paycheck-to-paycheck world and had hated the uncertainty of it.

As such, Penelope was careful with her purchases, knew when to pay for quality and when to abstain, and she was a saver. In the early days of her business, it had been especially hard. But if this wedding went off the way it should and brought her the recognition she anticipated, every penny she'd banked would be worth it because she'd finally, *blessedly,* be able to spend a bit of it as a down payment on a house.

A place of her own. Once she got into it, she'd never move again. With as many marriages as her parents had had, she'd been moving for what felt like her entire life, yanked from pillar to post, at the new stepparent's whim. She'd hated the packing and unpacking, sleeping in an unfamiliar place, making new friends, leaving old friends. But with her own house, bought and paid for with her own money that she'd earned, she'd never have to worry about that again.

Then again, given the threat aimed at Trent, that was a big if.

In fact, if she could get her hands on the interfering asshole who was making the threats, she'd throttle the culprit herself.

Of course, Trent and Nella's safety had to come before anything else. Still, she couldn't deny that the letter writer was throwing a wrench into more than a year's worth of planning.

It annoyed the hell out of her.

Penelope pulled into a parking space and took a deep cleansing breath, then let it go with a whoosh. It was after business hours, but she'd learned from Guy McCann that Seth McCutcheon had moved into the building today. Luckily, she'd gotten the security code to enter the building the last time she'd been by. She entered it now, then took the elevator to the third floor. To her chagrin, her palms inexplicably began to sweat, and a nervous flutter winged through her belly. She was being ridiculous, Pen told herself. He was only a man. There was no reason for her to be tense.

Her heels clicked in the quiet hallway, punctuating the rapid beat of her heart. She found his door and, after the briefest hesitation, she rang the bell. She heard the soft pad of bare feet over the floor, then the lock tumbled and he opened the door.

Whatever she'd expected, *he* was not it.

Penelope swallowed, blinked, and then attempted to pull *all* of him into focus. It was difficult, for many reasons, but the most pertinent was the fact that he was half-naked. He'd opened his door wearing nothing but a pair of low-slung khaki shorts that were in serious danger of slipping off his lean hips. His massive feet were indeed bare, as were most of his legs, all of his splendidly muscled chest, shoulders, back and neck. She caught a glimpse of a tattoo on his upper arm, but wasn't at an angle to appreciate it. A bottle of beer dangled loosely in one mouthwateringly large hand and the expression on his extraordinarily handsome face was baffled but friendly. A slow smile crept over a very sensual mouth and interest flared in his direct, dark green gaze.

Every cell in her body sizzled so loudly she actually thought she could hear the steam, and a flush of heat rolled over her skin in a long scorching wave that should have made fire flame from her fingertips.

Sweet mercy.

He peered out into the hall, then ducked back in and winced apologetically. "Listen, sweetheart, I'm not sure who sent you, but I don't need any company tonight."

Sent her? Company? It took almost three full seconds for the implication to set in, then another one to make her flush violently with embarrassment.

Another reason not to appear unexpectedly on someone's doorstep, Pen thought.

One might be mistaken for a hooker.

She extended her hand. "Penelope Hart," she said briskly. "I'm the—"

"Wedding planner," he finished, chuckling. "Sorry, I couldn't resist," he said, though she didn't get the impression he was sorry at all.

"That's okay. I get taken for a call girl all the time," she quipped.

He laughed, the sound low and slightly rough. Sexy. "My instructions said to meet you at eight tomorrow morning," he told her, opening the door to allow her in. She slid past him, too close to all that tempting bare masculine flesh, and felt a low throb hum a warning in her belly. She caught a faint whiff of his cologne, something smooth and musky. She licked her lips. "Did I miss a memo?"

"No," she said, turning as he closed the door. He motioned for her to follow him down a small hallway, then gestured for her to take a seat.

"Can I get you something to drink?" he asked. "Tea, soda, beer?"

Truthfully, she could use it—her mouth was bone-dry—but she ultimately refused. "No, thanks."

He excused himself for a minute and she took advantage of that time to take stock of his apartment. It had obviously been decorated by a man, but one with very good and very expensive taste. Heavy leather furniture the color of creamed coffee was positioned around a flat-panel television that hung above a marble fireplace and a large footlocker served as a coffee table. Various pieces of original artwork hung on the walls and a very interesting driftwood piece sat in the corner.

Though he'd supposedly only arrived today, already a few photographs were on the mantel and she resisted the urge to get up and inspect them. From this distance, she could make out one picture in particular—one of a family on a sailboat. She noted the condensation on the coaster on the table next to the recliner, a small bowl of trail mix beside it. The television was tuned into the History channel, a documentary about WWII paused, awaiting his return. A file with Trent McWilliam's name on it sat on the coffee table, along with a laptop, a gun and a set of keys. He might have only been here for twenty-four hours, but she could tell he'd made himself at home. Was he used to adapting quickly to his circumstances or was he happy to be here? she wondered, unreasonably intrigued.

"Sorry about that," he said, returning to the living room. He'd shrugged into a T-shirt, a dark olive that somehow made his eyes appear even greener, and had slipped on a pair of top-Siders.

Impossibly, he was just as good-looking with his shirt on. His hair was a dark brown with natural golden highlights and a small scar curved like a half-moon on his chin. Irrationally, she wanted to lick it. "No problem," she said, her voice strangely thick.

"Has something happened?" he asked.

She stared dumbly at him.

"With the case?" he prompted, his lips twitching. "Any new threat? Another letter? Anything suspicious going on? I'm assuming that's why you're here."

Yes, well. That was a perfectly logical assumption, but it'd be wrong. Because deciding to come over here was completely illogical. She was a moron, Penelope decided. A complete and utter moron.

"Actually, no," she said, clearing her throat. "I came by because I wanted to talk to you about our cover story."

His eyes twinkled and he passed a large hand over his face to disguise a smile. "Oh, I think you covered that quite well already. I read the dissertation, er, file."

Dissertation? So he was a smart-ass? How unfortunate that she liked that about him. "It's important that we have our story down," she said, tucking a strand of hair behind her ear. Jeez, it sounded even lamer when she said it aloud. What the hell had she been thinking?

"It is," he agreed. "Though I think we might have kept it a little simpler." He shrugged. "We met, we clicked, we're dating."

"That's too vague," Penelope told him, determined to

salvage this ill-advised visit. "Some of the women who are going to be at this wedding know me pretty well. We were sorority sisters and they're going to want details. How we met, where we went on our first date—"

"To Piedmont Park for a picnic," he supplied, evidently remembering some of what she'd supplied.

"—and what was it about you, specifically, that has made me want exclusivity rights."

"Nevertheless, I don't know why I had to rescue your puppy from a storm drain, why I'm taking art classes at night or why I have to be anti-meringue," he said. "I happen to like meringue. It's the perfect complement to chocolate pie." A small line emerged between his brows and that keen gaze, which upon first inspection had appeared irreverent, was actually more shrewd than what she'd originally given him credit for. "What do you mean 'make you want exclusivity rights'?"

"Rescuing the dog was noble, an admirable trait," she explained, ignoring his question. If someone rescued her own dog, Byron, she'd certainly find that noble. "You're taking the art classes because you aren't afraid to learn new things and you're anti-meringue, as you put it, because it's an endearing quirk."

"So I'm noble, intrepid and endearing?" he asked, his lips slipping into a wide smile. "Why don't I donate a kidney to a complete stranger so that I can be generous, too?"

"Ooh, that's a good one," she said. "You should write that down."

His expression blanked. "I was kidding."

She knew that, of course. "And you've got an excellent sense of humor, too. We're on a roll."

"You never answered my question."

"Which one?"

"Exclusivity rights? What did you mean?"

Penelope suddenly stood. She'd learned everything she needed to know and even more that she wished she hadn't. Like the fact that he was too damned good-looking for her own good, that he wasn't going to be as easily managed as she'd hoped and that he had enormous feet, which meant that the rest of him was probably proportionate. Heat flashed over her thighs and her lady business sizzled beneath her panties.

"We'll cover that in the morning," she said, slipping her purse over her shoulder. "I should be going. I've still got quite a bit to pull together before we roll out in the morning."

"Er...okay," he said, looking somewhat bemused, evidently unsure what to make of her or her unexpected visit. That was fair enough, she thought, because she was acting like a crazy person.

With a stream of silent obscenities and recriminations slipping through her brain, she retraced her steps to the door. She knew without looking that he was staring at her ass—she could practically feel his gaze—and then abruptly turned to tell him goodbye before reaching for the doorknob. Without warning, he bent down and kissed her. It was bold and brash, a sensual sweep of his lips over hers. Her breath caught in her throat, blood boiled beneath her skin and her heart faltered, then galloped in her chest.

Looking gallingly unaffected, he drew back and winked. "For practice," he said, his eyes twinkling with humor. She had a feeling he was trying to teach her some sort of lesson, but knew that she couldn't have earned a passing mark. Her brain was too scrambled to absorb any kind of message, well-intentioned or otherwise.

"Oh," she said, another brilliant stab at coherent conversation. She bade him a quick good-evening, then made a beeline for the elevator. He was still staring at her, a too-satisfied smile on his sexy lips, when the doors slid shut.

Penelope immediately sagged against the wall and let out a huge breath. Well, this was a fine snag. She'd had come here to find out if she was going to be able to pretend to like her bogus boyfriend and was leaving with the unequivocal assurance that, given the way her nipples were tingling and the breathless anticipation crowding her throat, she was in more danger of liking him *too much*. She smothered a whimper.

Something told her this wasn't going to be a good thing.

WEDDINGS BY HART was located a block off the historic Marietta Square in an old, white brick building with lots of black wrought-iron accessories. Window boxes burst with pink geraniums and an ornate sign with Penelope's logo hung over the door. The windows were loaded with wedding gowns, veils, tiaras and tulle, and just looking at them made Seth want to turn and run in the other direction.

Penelope was standing at the back of a big, white

van, a clipboard in her hand. Black curls spilled out of a ponytail that hung over her shoulder and she was nibbling on the end of a pencil, deep in thought.

He envied the pencil, especially since he knew how soft her mouth was. Kissing her last night had been a spur-of-the-moment decision—they were some of his best ones, if you asked him—and so he'd leaned in, catching her unaware. She'd been warm and responsive and when he'd tasted her sweet gasp, he'd felt something strangely expectant settle in his gut.

He'd done it in part to put her in her place, because he didn't think purposely mistaking her for a hooker had done the trick. Seth grinned, remembering the look on her face. He wanted her to know just exactly who was in charge here. Showing up at his place unannounced to scope him out and take his measure had been a ballsy move, he had to admit, but it had also been a power play. His company had been hired by Trent McWilliams to do a job and he'd been assigned to the case. She was supposed to cooperate with the security team, not try to run it. Undoubtedly, she just couldn't help herself—there was no way she could do her job effectively without being able to organize and delegate, he imagined—but this was *his* area of expertise.

"Morning," he said, handing her a cup of coffee. He stared at her, even more intrigued than he'd been last night. And that was saying something, because he'd gone over the file she'd given him at least half a dozen more times after she'd left his apartment, trying to glean as much as possible from what she'd included about herself.

She looked up and her startled gaze tangled with his. Her eyes were a clear blue, unpolluted and ringed in a slightly darker hue. A self-conscious smile flirted with her especially ripe lips, but never quite made the curl. "Good morning," she said, accepting the drink with a tiny frown.

"Two sugars, one cream, right?"

"Yes," she remarked hesitantly. She glanced at him uncertainly again. "How did you—"

Seth grinned. "You included it in the 'Things I Need To Know' section," he explained. As well as a lot of other interesting tidbits that hadn't seemed particularly pertinent before her visit, but had somehow gained significance. Like the fact that she was double-jointed, knew sign language, could recite "Casey at the Bat" and didn't like sweet potatoes. Why did any of this matter? He was still asking himself that, as well.

She inclined her head. "Ah. Thank you."

He glanced inside the van, where it had been packed with her luggage—purple, her favorite color, he remembered—and various wedding paraphernalia. "All packed up, then?"

"We will be as soon as your stuff is properly loaded."

He slid the duffel bag off his shoulder and directly into the van. "Done."

"What about that other bag?" she asked, nodding to his other arm.

"I need this one." It contained his laptop and files, all of which he needed to consult while they were on the road. He was as up to speed as he could be, but couldn't shake the feeling that he was missing something, that there was a clue hidden there that he just hadn't picked up on yet.

"And the other operatives?"

Operatives? She made them sound like international spies, Seth thought, feeling his lips twitch. "They're going to meet us in Foley and follow us in." Actually, they'd originally planned to meet here, but Forrester had wanted to go to Lambert's Café, "Home of the throwed rolls" and had convinced the other two men to leave a little bit early this morning so that they could have lunch.

"No problem," she said. "I'd actually promised my staff that we'd stop at Lambert's on the way in, so that'll be perfect."

Unable to help himself, he chuckled.

"What's so funny?"

"That's why the other guys left early. They didn't think we'd have time to stop."

She slipped the pencil behind her ear and then closed the van doors. "We always have time to stop for yeast rolls," she said. "I built it into the schedule."

She would. "This must be one helluva restaurant," Seth remarked with a shake of his head.

She arched a brow. "You've never been?"

"No," he said.

Truth be told, he'd never been to the Gulf Shores area at all. Several of the kids from his high school class had gone down after graduation, but he'd already had a job lined up and, even with the ROTC scholarship, still needed every penny he could get. He'd stayed home and his mother had thrown a big party for him. She'd cooked his favorite meal—chicken and dumplings—and they'd had a horror film marathon, then played cards. She'd let him win a hundred bucks from her and wouldn't take it back no matter how hard he'd tried to return it to her. Afterward they'd gone out to Donagan Lake and gone sailing, which had been one of his mother's favorite pastimes. He smiled, remembering, and felt a hollow ache settle around his heart.

Her expression brightened. "Oh well, you're in for a treat then. It's good, old country food and lots of it."

That certainly sounded good to him, Seth thought. He offered to drive, knowing that she would refuse. This was a woman who had written a ten-page history of their *fake* relationship and dropped by his apartment twelve hours before they were supposed to meet just to scope him out. The term "control freak" didn't begin to cover her need to direct, organize and otherwise oversee.

He'd gotten the distinct impression that his way of doing things with a more fluid plan was going to drive her insane.

Perversely, he actually looked forward to that.

"I've got it, thanks," she said, then promptly slid into the driver's seat and waited expectedly on him.

He felt a droll smile roll around his lips as he settled into the passenger seat and watched her drop her sunglasses into place. She picked up a walkie-talkie and told Monica—her good friend and assistant who'd been with her for the past three years—that they were leaving. She waited for a response, then pulled out into traffic. Paul, her other must-have-man on staff, was the official heavy lifter and had only been around for about a year. He'd been in the service, but hadn't re-upped after his first four years. He had to give the guys at Ranger Security credit—they'd left no stone unturned and had thoroughly investigated everyone.

"So you've had a chance to look over everything?" she asked.

"I'd looked over everything before you came by last night to check up on me," Seth told her. "I thought I passed the test last night."

"Who said anything about a test?"

"You didn't have to." He settled his own sunglasses into place and tried not to stare at the sleek expanse of tanned thigh her sundress revealed. "Did I pass muster? Can I be your pretend boyfriend?" he teased.

"We've got a lot riding on whether or not you can act like my boyfriend," she said, not bothering to deny it. "Sorry if my concern annoys you, but I just needed to make sure that you—"

"Would be someone you'd date," he finished, chuckling. "I get it. So?" he prodded, purposely goading her because it was fun. "Are you going to be able to muster the enthusiasm to pretend to like me?"

She flushed, the pink climbing her neck. "I think I can manage." She pulled onto 75 south, competently negotiating the heavy morning traffic. "What about you? Going to have any problem playing the part of Mr. Wedding Planner?"

His gaze lingered over her leg, up over her breasts and settled on her mouth. Given the dream he'd had last night, one that featured the two of them rolling naked in the sand, he didn't think so. "No," he said, his voice strangely hoarse. "I think I can manage it. Granted, it helps that you're attractive." He sighed heavily. "Feigning interest in a dog-pointer would have been a harder sell."

"That's a terrible thing to say," she said, trying to turn a shocked laugh into self-righteous outrage. She didn't succeed and, to his delight, continued to smile.

"Terribly honest," he corrected, pleased that he'd startled a chuckle out of her. He shot her a modest grin. "That's the least you can expect from a noble puppy-rescuer, right?"

"But you never really rescued a puppy."

"Do you want me to get confused? I'm trying to get into character here."

She sighed heavily and bit her lip. "Why do I get the feeling I'm going to bitterly regret coming up with our history?"

Probably because she was, Seth thought. But she couldn't have it both ways. She either wanted him to adhere to the script or she didn't. And, as much as he'd originally dreaded this, he could actually see that pretending to be her boyfriend was going to be the silver lining of this assignment. He was intensely—stupidly— interested in her. For every question she'd answered about herself, he had twenty more.

Starting with the one she hadn't answered last night. He'd been turning that "exclusivity rights" comment of hers over and over again in his mind. The more he thought about it, the more it sounded to him as if she'd never found someone she cared enough about to give them exclusivity. Like she'd never really had a significant other.

But that couldn't be right, Seth thought, shooting her a covert look. She was a wedding planner, for heaven's sake. From death do you part, to love and to cherish, in sickness and in health, I do and I do. She *arranged* romance.

"Back to that exclusivity comment you made last night," Seth persisted, unwilling to let it go. Intuition told him a wealth of information was hidden in that offhand little comment and he wanted to know what it was.

From the corner of his eye he saw her hands tense on the steering wheel and her sleek jaw tighten. She lifted her chin. "What about it?"

"What did you mean? Because unless I'm mistaken, the inference was that you giving exclusivity to someone was a rare occurrence, a phenomenon of sorts. Or did I read that wrong?" He chuckled under his breath. "I mean it almost sounds like you've never had a boyfriend before."

Her cheeks puffed as she exhaled mightily. "That's because I haven't," she said. "By choice. I'm in the business of uniting couples, Mr. McCutcheon. It doesn't mean I'm in the business of *becoming* one."

And with that grim, enigmatic statement, which hadn't been in the file—hers or Ranger Security's—Penelope Hart, the commitment-phobic wedding planner suddenly became the most interesting person Seth had ever met.

4

FROM THE LOOK on his face, she'd thoroughly shocked him, Pen thought and was secretly pleased. For whatever reason, she got the impression that very little surprised Seth McCutcheon. By doing so, she'd accomplished something rare.

Nevertheless, a subject change was in order. She was already at a disadvantage, thanks to the unexpected, unholy attraction tying her middle up in knots. Giving him more personal information about her when she knew so very little about him wasn't prudent. The flow of information hadn't been the least bit equitable and she had no one to blame for that but herself.

In retrospect, coming up with their history and providing him with so much personal information, even if most of it was superficial, had turned out to be one of her less intelligent ideas. She should have met him first, then put together what he would need, not the other way around. But how was she to know that he was going to be the most attractive man she'd ever seen. Or that her loins quivered just by looking at him. Or that he was in possession of a very keen mind and eyes that she suspected never missed a trick?

"So now that you've reviewed the case file, do you have a particular suspect in mind?" she asked. She picked up 285 west and took a sip of her coffee.

"Other than safely assuming it's a woman, no," he admitted.

She thought so, too, but still felt the irrational need to argue. She suspected it was going to become the theme for the weekend. "What makes you so sure it's a woman?"

From the corner of her eye she watched him grin. "I'm not maligning your gender, Penelope," he said, and she loved the way her name came off his lips. "It's just simple deductive reasoning. Trent's a good-looking guy about to go off the market. As you know, he got dozens of letters from disappointed women."

"There were a few from men, too," she retorted. Mostly gay men, she would admit, but still...

"True," he said. "But when you consider the ratios and the whole passive-aggressive nature of the threats...I'm not saying that I don't think it's real or that this person isn't dangerous, because I do." He frowned. "But I'm getting a weird vibe on this, as though there's something I'm missing, a dot I'm not connecting."

"You haven't even really started yet," Pen added.

"I know, but—" He shook his head. "At any rate, my money is on this being a woman. Typically, a man's nature is to confront, put it all out in the open and come to blows if necessary. Women tend to be a bit more... sneaky." He pulled a face. "They'll bake chocolate laxatives into brownies, slash tires, scrub the toilet bowl with a guy's toothbrush. That sort of thing."

She felt a laugh break up in her throat. "Are you speaking from personal experience?"

"No," he said. His expression turned thoughtful. "Though I did once have a girl place an ad for free goats in the local newspaper, using my number for the contact."

She chuckled darkly, admittedly impressed.

He swiveled to look at her, his green eyes crinkling at the corners. Half of his mouth kicked up in a smile that made her pulse jump. Good Lord, he was beautiful. Need warmed in her belly, making her squirm in her seat. "Filing that one away for future use, are you?"

"I have to admit I kind of like it. Little effort for a very annoying payoff." She bit her bottom lip. "What did you do?"

"What do you mean, what did I do?" he asked, shooting her a look. "I told every bleeding caller that I didn't have any free goats, then I started giving them *her* number."

He would, she thought, chuckling. "No, I meant, what did you do to her? The woman who placed the ad?"

He winced. "Oh. I gave her the it's-not-you-it's-me line," he said with a sheepish shrug. "I was just trying to spare her feelings. It would have been unkind to tell her that she was too needy and her laugh made me think of a braying donkey."

She felt her mouth drop open and another burst of laughter rolled off her tongue. "You think?" He was utterly outrageous and equally honest. She found that she liked that about him, that it was, in many ways, very refreshing.

"I was trying to be a gentleman," he said. "It wasn't my fault she went all *Fatal Attraction* on me."

"How long had you been seeing her?"

"About three hours. Dinner and a movie. And at the end of it, rather than lie to her and tell her I'd had a good time or would give her a call, I cut to the chase to keep her from developing any expectations." He shook his head. "I'd have been better off lying to her, but it's not my style. I can't abide a liar."

That sounded personal, Pen thought, noting the grim tone of his voice. That tone piqued her curiosity and she shot him a sidelong glance. "Me, either," she said. She waited a beat and asked the one question that had been burning on her tongue since the minute he'd started this story. "So, you're obviously not married, otherwise your boss wouldn't have paired you up with me. Any close calls?" she asked, purposely making the question light.

He turned to look at her then, a knowing twinkle in his eye. Half of his sinfully wicked mouth cocked up in a smile. "No," he told her. And that was all. He didn't elaborate, didn't offer the first insight into why that was the case.

But considering she hadn't either, she could hardly fault him, could she?

Which was why he was being purposely vague.

Naturally that made her all the more curious about him. But rather than press him for an explanation—

because she knew he'd expect her to return in kind—she merely smiled.

"You've been working with Trent and Nella for more than a year, right?" he asked.

"I have."

"And you're familiar with the guest list and everyone involved on a more personal level with the wedding?"

That would be true also. She nodded. "Yes."

"So have you been getting any weird or negative vibes from anyone? Her mother? His mother? Brides-maids?"

Though she typically made it a rule not to discuss her opinions of any member of the wedding party or their friends and family—it was a small world, after all, and she'd never wanted to risk saying anything that could potentially harm her business—in this instance, she didn't see how she was going to adhere to that principle.

Still, she hesitated, because it felt like a betrayal of sorts. Her couples came to her, asking her to provide the setting and experience for one of the most monumental events in their lives—their marriage. Admitting that the bride's mother was a total bitch or the groom's father was a skinflint felt wrong, even if the descriptions were true.

"Whatever you say stays with the security team," Seth told her. "It goes no further. But you have the most access and you've more than likely already interacted with the person responsible."

She imagined that was true as well, as unsettling as it was. Penelope released a breath. "Nella's mother is overjoyed, so I think we can safely rule her out. Ordinarily the mother of the bride ends up being a pain in the ass. They have a specific idea of what they want their little girl to look like on her wedding day and are loath to give it up. Very often, I end up having to tangle with the mother on behalf of the bride. It's *her* day. Period. Nella's mother hasn't been like that at all. She's simply wanted whatever is going to make Nella happy." She sighed again. "Trent's mother, on the other hand, doesn't seem as taken with Nella as Nella's mother is with Trent. However, before you make anything out of that, that's typically the case, as well. Have you ever heard the old saying 'A daughter's a daughter for life, but a son is only a son until he takes a wife'?"

He shook his head.

"Well, in my experience that's been pretty true. Even the biggest mama's boy doesn't need her as much after he's married."

"So Trent's a mama's boy?"

"Trent adores his mother and respects her opinion, but he doesn't let her direct him in any way. That bodes well for Nella, because you can tell a lot about how a man is going to treat a wife based on how he treats his mother."

He turned to look at her. "Really?"

"Yes," she said. "It sounds trite, but it's true. A mother is every guy's first frame of reference for a woman. He either loves and respects her—appreciates her—or he doesn't."

"And based on that, you can tell how he's going to treat his wife?"

"Not in all circumstances," she said. "But just as a rule, you know?"

He seemed genuinely intrigued. "And you've seen this?"

"I've coordinated more than two-hundred-fifty weddings over the past five years. I'd say it holds true around ninety percent of the time."

He hummed under his breath. "Impressive odds. So do you think Trent's mother could be behind this, then?"

Penelope took a second to really think about it, to check her gut. In all truth, she couldn't say that she especially liked Trent's mother, who was a little on the chilly side, but did she think she'd risk wrecking Trent's wedding when Trent was so obviously happy? So in love with Nella? Ultimately…no.

She shook her head. "I really don't think so. In the end Trent's happiness is more important to her than anything else. I think she has doubts as to whether Nella will make him happy in the long run, but he believes she will. Mrs. McWilliams is not going to interfere, to risk the rift."

"Do you think Nella will make Trent happy in the long run?"

That was a question she hadn't expected. She turned to look at him, then back to the road. "Does that matter?"

"I'm just curious, that's all. You seem to have a real knack for reading people."

She did, actually, which had helped make her really good at her job. That he'd noticed made her chest swell.

"I think Trent and Nella are going to be very happy for a very long time. There's a mutual respect there, a reverence, even, that I don't often see. They're a nine."

He frowned. "A nine?"

Shit. She shouldn't have said that. "It's nothing," she said, wishing she could cut her own tongue out. "It's just a little scale I use."

"On your couples?" he pressed. "You rate them? On whether or not they're going to live happily ever after?"

She cleared her throat. "As for the rest of the bridal party, all of Nella's bridesmaids are happy for her," she said, trying to get back to their original subject. "She's only got four and, with the exception of Trent's sister, Lucy, she's known all of them since grade school."

"But if you don't think they're going to make it, then how do you give your dead-level best to make it wonderful for them?" he continued, still stuck on her rating system. "Why bother?"

"Because it's *their* day—it's what *they* want—and it's my job. It doesn't matter what I think. It's not about me. It's about them. And really, who am I to judge? To interfere?"

"Especially when you don't want to risk it yourself," he said, nodding sagely, as if he'd just cracked her own secret code. "I get it."

She chuckled darkly and bit the end of her tongue, a forcible reminder to keep her mouth shut. He was trying to goad her, to get her to tell him why she'd never wanted a boyfriend and, by extension, a wedding of her own. Had she ever fantasized about it? Yes, she had. She was a wedding planner, after all. She knew that she'd want a cake covered in fondant, a simple gown and even simpler veil, and lots and lots of calla lilies. She imagined the party—the dancing, the twinkling lights, the food—but she'd never once imagined a groom.

And if that wasn't telling, then she didn't know what was. That was self-preservation in its most potent form, her subconscious telling her that it wasn't meant to be.

She took the exit for 85 south and grimly noted they had another five hours alone in the car before the show would fully commence. He'd probably kiss her again, Pen thought, and felt a thrill whip through her at the mere thought.

And for the first time in her life, Penelope Hart thought she might be in over her head.

It looked like another subject change was in order.

"I UNDERSTAND this is your first assignment for Ranger Security, that you're new to the agency," Penelope said, playing defense again.

He'd give her credit—she was damned good at it.

Every time he tried to edge the needle toward something a little personal, she'd invariably turn the conversation back to him or to the case. But never about herself and her inability or desire to commit. The incongruity was utterly fascinating.

She fascinated him.

He suspected that he couldn't afford to be fascinated by her. Even though he'd found himself staring at her beautiful mouth and imagining the depraved things she could do with it to him, he seriously needed to keep his priorities in check.

He was here to catch an instigator, to possibly prevent a murder. He'd do well to remember that.

"That's right," Seth told her. He didn't elaborate. If she wanted to know more, she was going to have to ask. He suspected this was going to be the pattern for both of them and smiled at the thought. He'd bet she was damned good at chess.

He watched her release a small sigh, her lips twitching with put-upon humor. "And what were you doing before you became a security expert."

Was it terrible of him to enjoy this so much? He cocked his head thoughtfully. "I guess you could say I was in a similar field."

He could sense her frustration building. "And who was your previous employer?"

"Uncle Sam."

She aahed knowingly. "You were in the military?"

"Yes."

"What branch?"

"Army."

Something clicked in her quick little brain and he watched her smile. "A Ranger?"

"That's right."

"How long did you serve?"

"Eight years."

She gave a slow nod. "Thank you for your service."

He hadn't expected that. The surprise comment left him momentarily at a loss. He swallowed. "You're welcome," he finally managed to say.

"One of my stepdads was in the military," she explained. "He was in the army, too. A warrant officer. I never fully understood the sacrifice, both for the soldiers and their families until then. It gave me a whole new understanding and appreciation for our men and women in uniform."

One of her stepdads? How many had she had? he wondered, suspecting that this little tidbit was somehow vitally important. His own mother had never remarried after his father had walked out—bastard, Seth thought. He hadn't been joking when he said he couldn't abide a liar.

Though he'd only been five when his father had left, Seth distinctly remembered her believing that the man was going to come back. He remembered her worrying about his father, convinced that he'd been in an accident, that he'd been hurt. She'd walked the floor, called the police and filed a missing person's report as soon as they'd let her. The bastard had told her he was going to the store for gallon of ice cream—it had been unbearably hot that summer—and he'd simply never come back. He hadn't written, hadn't called, hadn't made any sort of contact with them ever again.

Seth had waited until he'd graduated from college before tracking the man down. He'd found him some fifty miles away, shacked up with a girl half his age in a ratty little trailer park. "Do you know who I am?" he'd asked his father, rage boiling up inside of him. He hadn't gone there with the express intention of hurting him, but he'd taken one look at the man who'd abandoned his family and hurt his mother and an anger like he'd never known had rolled through him and he'd…snapped. "I'm your son," he'd told him, then proceeded to beat the living hell out of him. The girlfriend had called the police and, rather than let his mother post bail, Seth had spent the night in jail. Had he cared?

Not in the slightest.

A man was supposed to keep his word, to keep his promises.

"You were in Iraq?" Penelope asked, yanking him away from his thoughts.

He gave himself a mental shake. "I've been there, too, but up until two weeks ago, I was in Afghanistan," he said, letting go a small breath. It still felt wrong being here, Seth thought. As though this was not his real life and he was merely standing in for someone else. It felt odd living alone, waking up in the morning without a specific purpose and plan for the day. Granted the plan might change at the drop of a hat, especially if he was in charge, but the purpose never did.

And it was too damned quiet. It had bugged him so much he'd started leaving the television on all the time, just to simulate conversation. He'd gotten a call from Finn a couple of nights ago and just hearing his friend's voice, listening to the sound of rowdy soldiers in the background, had made his throat go tight.

But he'd promised.

Because he didn't want the burden of his unhappiness hanging over his sister's head, he'd never confided the circumstances of his return, though he knew she suspected. She called every day and always put Mitchell on the phone to relay some sort of gooey greeting. Did he think they needed him? Yes, he actually did. His sister had had a hard row to hoe since Rat Bastard had left her and he imagined the betrayal was especially painful in light of her son. Coupled with the loss of their mother— their constant—it had been especially terrible for her.

He knew Katie was second-guessing her choices and was having trouble making decisions, fearing to make the wrong one again. He hated seeing his otherwise happy, confident little sister reduced to this tired, chronic uncertainty, but other than being available when she wanted to talk, he didn't know what else he could do for her. His mother thought being there would be enough—and she would know after his own father's desertion. He certainly hoped she'd been right.

Because she was going to miss so many milestones, his mother had written letters to each of her children and to Mitchell to be opened upon the occasions she'd indicated. She'd given Katie's letters to him and his letters to Katie.

She'd handed him the first when he'd arrived home.

It had been simple enough. A thank-you for coming out of the military, an apology for forcing his hand, an order to take care of his sister and Mitchell, an assurance that all would ultimately be well. "I know it doesn't feel like it now," she'd written. "But this will be good. You'll find your rudder…and I hope she initially mops the deck with you."

His gaze slid to the woman sitting in the driver's seat and he felt a curious whirring sensation bolt through his chest. If he let her close enough, he knew beyond a shadow of a doubt that the woman seated next to him could do that, Seth thought. He didn't know where the assurance came from but felt it all the same. How bizarre, particularly when he'd never had this sort of reaction to a woman before. He'd never felt anything remotely resembling this intense curiosity, hellfire attraction and certain inexplicable knowledge that she was different, dangerous even, if he let her get too close.

The picture of efficiency, Penelope was dressed in a sleeveless pale green dress that accentuated her curvy frame and contrasted well with her dark hair. She wore a pair of dangly silver earrings, a silver necklace with a single *P* charm and sparkly silver flip-flops on her small feet. Pale pink nail polish decorated her toes, along with what looked like little palm trees painted on each of her big toes. She looked relaxed yet competent, but that self-assuredness was only a small part of her appeal. She was effortlessly sexy and fresh, interesting and smart, and he wanted to lick her up like an ice-cream cone while she melted all over him.

Though he imagined he could kiss her again as part of the ruse—and he fully intended to—he seriously doubted he'd be able to justify any further salacious contact. Pity, that, he thought, feeling his dick twitch in his pants.

He wanted her.

It was inconvenient, foolhardy, utterly inappropriate and damned poor timing, but there it was.

"What made you decide to leave the military?" she finally asked, evidently unable to help herself.

"What makes you think the decision was mine?"

"Are you saying it wasn't?"

He chuckled and looked out the window, watching the passing landscape with more fascination than was warranted.

"You can always tell me it's none of my business," she said, a smile in her voice. "I'm just curious. Typically you Special Forces guys don't go in with the intent to come out until you retire. You've had too much training, too much of your life assigned to a particular purpose. You're what? Thirty-two?"

"Yes."

"Aha!" she chortled, as though this was a contest. "Got you to answer one directly." She gave a little fist pump that made him grin.

"I'll answer as directly as you like, so long as the favor is returned in kind." He purposely let his gaze linger along her neck, waiting for it to pinken. It did. "And I think you have more to hide."

"I don't have anything to hide," she said, immediately refuting his charge.

"So you're purposely mysterious?"

Her eyes widened and she smothered another laugh. "Purposely mysterious? I think you're giving me too much credit. I seriously doubt I'm that interesting."

That's where she'd be wrong. She was fascinating. "I'd have to disagree with you on that one," he said, and had the pleasure of watching her swallow. The tops of her ears turned red.

She snorted. "You'd disagree with me if I said the sky was blue if it meant you wouldn't have to answer a direct question."

"Hi, Pot. Meet Kettle," he said in a deadpan tone.

She merely chuckled. "Diverted again. But I still haven't forgotten what I asked you."

She wouldn't. He released a small sigh. "You want to know why I came out of the military?"

"That's what I've been asking."

"The short answer is I lost a bet in a card game."

She mulled that over. "That's definitely a short answer. You're not the type to bet your future on a card game."

"How do you know?"

"Intuition," she said. "You'd lose money before you'd lose control. Are you going to tell me the long story?"

She'd known him less than twelve hours and had pegged that right already. What else was she going to correctly guess before this assignment was over? Seth wondered, feeling a bit unnerved. What other truths had her keen mind already deduced? He waited a beat, debating. "It's a sad one," he finally told her.

She instantly winced and muttered a low oath. "I'm sorry," she said, immediately contrite. "I had no right to pry."

"The question was reasonable," he said, sensing her discomfort. "I'm working on a case with you that impacts your future and the future of your clients. I'm untested. An unknown quantity." He laughed softly. "If I were you, I'd have questions, too."

She shook her head. "Nevertheless, I shouldn't have pressed it. You don't owe me an explanation. Trent's people have hired you and they're confident that you'll take care of him. That's good enough for me. I was just more curious than anything. We're going to be spending a great deal of time together over the next three days and I just thought it would be better if we knew a little bit about each other. I—"

"I kept a promise," he finally told her. "And so I'm here."

She looked strangely moved. She swallowed, then gave a jerky nod and managed a magnanimous smile. "Well, that's even better than saving a puppy from a storm drain."

Seth chuckled, thankful that the moment had passed. "I'm glad you approve."

And he was, which was clue enough that her opinion already mattered more to him than it should.

5

AFTER WHAT HAD FELT like the longest car ride in the history of the world, Penelope was still feeling strangely fidgety and out of sorts hours later. Despite the fact that she'd been putting out fires most of the day and was completely in her element doing so, she'd nevertheless been keenly aware of *him*. She didn't have to look to know that he was talking with another one of the Ranger Security guys—Will Forrester, if memory served, another tall drink of water.

She could *feel* him there, ten feet to her left.

To make matters worse, she could feel it even more when he looked at her. It was as though a mere glance in her direction raised some sort of supersensory perception in her brain and, when that purely masculine gaze roamed over her, whether long and lingering or short and fleeting, she could feel that, too.

It was disconcerting to say the least.

"I think every guest should get a matching tattoo, don't you? How about little dolphins jumping through wedding bands? Wouldn't that be adorable? I'll line someone up to take care of that *tout de suite*."

Pen blinked and looked at her friend and assistant, Monica. The petite blonde had come to work for her fresh out of college and had quickly proven herself to be not only a good friend, but an invaluable asset to her business. She was a little mouthy and even more opinionated and she didn't always have the best judgment in men, but she was a hard worker who never failed to give Penelope more than one-hundred-and-ten percent.

"What?" Pen asked, trying at least that hard to focus.

Monica heaved an exasperated sigh, her spiky blond curls quivering in irritation. "You haven't been listening to a word I've said!" she accused. "You didn't bat a lash when I mentioned squirting disappearing ink all over Nella's gown or clubbing Trent over the head with a candelabra and dragging him off for myself. What's wrong with you?" She gasped and her gaze turned annoyingly shrewd. "Oh, never mind. It's your *boyfriend*," she drawled with enough innuendo to make Penelope blush.

"Pretend boyfriend," she corrected. She bit her bottom lip. "He is a bit more distracting than I'd anticipated," she admitted.

Monica glanced over and slid Seth an appraising look, one that unreasonably irritated Pen. "I'll say," her assistant breathed. "Pity he's the only single one, isn't it? They're all damned fine."

It was true, she had to admit. She couldn't imagine that being handsome was prerequisite to landing a job with the elite firm, but if not, then they'd gotten terribly lucky. All four of the guys representing Ranger Security were unbelievably attractive and, in some sort of bizarre twist of irony, Seth McCutcheon was the one who appealed to her the most.

There was something about the shape of his smile, the hint of perpetual laughter and irreverence lurking in his dark green gaze that made him especially attractive. She liked the way the sun glinted off the golden hairs on his beautifully muscled forearms and the competent strength in his hands. He was loose and easy in his own skin and had an effortless self-assurance that was as inherent as breathing. It was hard to be unmoved by that sort of confidence and she was anything but unmoved.

In fact, if she had to sum up her present state in one word it would be *hot.*

Of course, it would have helped if he hadn't slipped so easily into character the instant they'd arrived on the island. The minute they'd gotten out of the car, he'd immediately taken her hand, threading his fingers through hers, and the feel of his rough palm against hers—the mere strength in his fingers—had sent a knife of desire right through her. The lust alone she could deal with. It was familiar, even if this was a more concentrated form of it. But it was the sudden longing, this strange sense of something more… That completely unnerving awareness was making her feel she could vibrate out of her own skin.

It wasn't exactly what one could call an altogether pleasant sensation.

And, thanks to the red-letter terrorist—her own personal nickname for the thoughtless asshole casting a pall on the wedding preparations—there wasn't truly an end in sight.

In order to keep Seth as close to Trent and Nella as possible without actually raising suspicions, she and Seth had been given the guesthouse at the back of the property. In just a few short minutes, they were going to be alone together for the rest of the night. If she didn't get herself under control, self-combustion was going to become a legitimate concern.

"So what do you think, boss? Can we call it a day?"

No doubt her intrepid assistant and the rest of her crew were eager to scope out the local nightlife. Under ordinary circumstances she might have been, too, but Penelope had too much riding on the outcome of this wedding to muck it up with some premature partying. She was keen to find out what Seth had learned since he'd gotten here, to see if anything else had happened. His comment on the drive down that she'd probably already interacted with the perpetrator had given her a lot to think about today.

Pen consulted her clipboard and ultimately nodded her consent. "I think we've got everything under control," she said.

"We're prowling for good seafood and margaritas," Monica told her, and jerked her head in Seth's direction. "You and Mr. Gorgeous are welcome to join us."

"He's got to stay close to Trent and Nella," Pen reminded her. Monica was the only staff member that she'd confided in regarding the threat to the bride and groom. While the others suspected something strange was going on, they hadn't been brought into the loop. In fact, even Trent and Nella's families had been left in the dark. The less said, the less likely the real letter-writer would be tipped off to Ranger Security's presence.

"And you've got to stay close to him," she said, nodding sagely. "Poor you."

"Shut up," Pen hissed, shooting a covert look at Seth. "What's everyone saying?"

"About him and your sudden penchant for bringing boyfriends to work? Not a lot, actually," she said. "They don't completely buy the Seth's-a-big-Trent-McWilliams-fan line, but they have too much respect for you to call you an outright liar, either."

That was good, she supposed, Pen thought.

"Paul was the most surprised. He didn't think Seth was your type."

Penelope couldn't imagine Seth not being anyone's type.

She frowned, momentarily sidetracked. Paul, a friend of Monica's, had been working for her for a little less than a year. He was hardworking and funny and, though she wished he wouldn't smoke, provided endless entertainment. "Paul thinks I have a type?"

"Yep. He calls them the E.D.'s."

"The Erectile Dysfunctions?" She grimaced. "That's rather harsh."

Monica snickered. "Not Erectile Dysfunctions," she said, laughing softly. "The Easily Directed. Paul says the only kind of man you ever date is the kind you can boss around. Somehow he doesn't think your current 'boyfriend' fits the mold."

That's because Seth McCutcheon was more accustomed to giving orders than taking them, Pen thought, releasing a shaky breath. "I don't only date men I can boss around," she said, because at the very least, she needed to refute the charge.

"Yes, you do," Monica told her. "But that's just because you're smarter than the rest of us." She nudged her shoulder indulgently. "See you in the morning."

And with that parting comment, her assistant made her exit.

Seconds later, Nella joined her. Looking more relaxed than any bride she'd ever known, her former sorority sister surveyed the scene and a dimple winked in her cheek. "I know I don't have to ask, but how is everything coming together?"

Pen smiled. "Perfectly," she said, though that wasn't exactly true. Somehow or another, when she'd called to double-check the times with the caterer, she'd been told that their order had been canceled. Er…no. "You have absolutely nothing to worry about."

"Apart from the whole someone wanting to commit murder—possibly mine or my future husband's—you mean?" she teased.

"Apart from that, yes," Pen said, glad her friend could find a bit of humor in the situation. But that was Nella. She'd always been able to find a laugh in just about anything. It was no small part of her friend's charm.

"It's beautiful here," Nella sighed, looking out toward the bay. "Trent's sister tried every way in the world to convince us to marry in a church or a hotel—anywhere with air-conditioning—but this is Trent's favorite place on earth. He says he feels more grounded and content here than he does anywhere else. When he first told me about the house, I'd imagined a huge mansion dwarfing the trees and lots of modern art, compliments of his interior decorator." She gave a grin. "Instead, it's more cottage than mansion, with local art on the walls and more screened-in porches and deck than house. I absolutely love it here," she said. "Probably not more than Trent does," she confided. "But just as much." She slid Penelope a sly look. "Can I tell you a secret?"

"Of course."

"Greece is a ruse."

"What?"

She looked around to make sure no one was eavesdropping, then leaned in closer. "We're not going to Greece for our honeymoon."

"You're not?"

"No. We're coming back here. We're simply leaving long enough for everyone else to clear out, then we're honeymooning here, in the place we're going to call home. We haven't—" Nella faltered. "We've waited," she said, blushing to the roots of her hair. "And when we finally…well…we want to be here, at home." She smiled self-consciously. "Sounds bizarre, doesn't it? I'm marrying a man who can afford to take me all over the world and the only place I care about being with him is home."

For whatever reason, Penelope's throat grew tight and her gaze inexplicably drifted to Seth. She made herself look away. "I don't think it sounds bizarre at all," she said. "It sounds like the two of you can't wait to start your life together and what better place than where you'll have your happiest moments? You're making this about what you want, not what everyone expects, and that's wonderful, Nella. I'm so incredibly happy for you."

"Do you think Seth is going to be able to prevent a tragedy here, if it comes to that?" she asked, betraying the first bit of nerves.

"Without a doubt," Pen told her. She didn't know where her sense of certainty came from, but she knew it all the same. She'd known Seth less than twenty-four hours but she would have had the same conviction had it only been twenty-four seconds. He inspired that kind of confidence, that kind of unquestioning regard. He'd signed on to neutralize the threat and protect Trent and Nella at all costs and she instinctively knew he'd put himself in harm's way before he'd let something happen to them.

I kept a promise, he'd said.

Four simple words, but the intent and act behind them spoke volumes about his character. Seth McCutcheon was one of those rare men who actually did what he said he was going to do. He was a man of his word and, in a world where lies were more common than the truth, where everyone was content to do the right thing until it became uncomfortable, that was a very, very admirable quality.

She suspected it was just the first of many she was going to discover about her *pretend* boyfriend.

But if she had to have a pretend boyfriend, she could certainly do a lot worse.

SHE WAS LOOKING at him again, Seth thought, feeling a telltale twitch in his pants. He'd been semiaroused since the instant he'd seen her nibbling on the end of that pencil this morning and, predictably, five hours in the car hadn't helped matters. He didn't know what sort of perfume she was wearing—something musky with a hint of exotic spice—but it was absolutely driving him crazy. Every once in a while he'd catch a whiff of it and it would sort of stun him, leaving him momentarily dazed and out of sorts.

He wasn't accustomed to feeling either of those things, especially where a woman was concerned.

That this one was poised to knock him off his game was irritating at best and downright stupid at worst. He couldn't afford to be anything short of one-hundred-percent focused. Trent and Nella's safety depended on his attention to every detail, to not missing a single nuance of what was happening around him. It was a skill that had served him well in the military and would no doubt be helpful on this mission, as well. Like now, for instance.

There were three men installing the dance floor beneath the largest tent, which was currently being festooned with little white lights. Twenty feet northeast of where he stood, Trent, his mother and sister were talking and, though he couldn't hear a word, a quick read of the body language told him Trent's mother was trying to direct. Trent was standing firm with an eye toward his future bride and his sister was twirling her hair around her finger as though merely clocking time. Ten feet to his right, Penelope and Nella were chatting amiably about something that was making Nella smile. From the corner of his eye, he couldn't discern the exact look on Pen's face, but it was one that was hauntingly puzzling, a combination of surprise and wistfulness.

He was entirely too interested in what had caused that expression, Seth realized, muttering a hot curse under his breath.

Acting as one of the tent company's crew, Tanner made his way over. "We're going to head out," he said, shooting a look down toward the water. The sun was sinking low on the bay, casting orange iridescent shadows on the waves, and a line of squawking seagulls sat perched along the end of the pier. The salty breeze ruffled through the palms and stirred the Spanish moss dripping from the live oaks. It was a beautiful close to a long day though Seth suspected the coming evening was going to test limits he hadn't known were there.

Seth nodded. "You guys were lucky to have been able to rent a house just a couple of doors down," he remarked, thankful that the security team would be on the island instead of having to move off-site like the rest of the wedding crew.

Tanner merely grinned. "Lucky to have a boss with friends in high places."

Given the fact that Payne owned the building in which the agency was currently housed, Seth suspected their boss had lots of friends in high places. "There is that," he said, nodding.

"What's your gut saying on this?" Tanner asked him. "Any thoughts?"

Seth released a slow breath and rubbed his hand over

the back of his neck. His gut was sending him mixed signals, which was a first. He suspected that the threats were merely a stall tactic, but he couldn't shake the sensation that there really was something brewing here, something more sinister. But were they related? That was the million-dollar question.

"Well, given what we know regarding the people who sent the save-the-date and wedding invitations, it's someone who is close. Probably closer than we realize," he said. "They've made threats but no other overt action that we know of." He winced. "Intuition tells me that there's no real threat to Trent and Nella, that the irrational tone of the notes was to postpone the wedding, to keep Trent on the market a little longer. But...I don't know. Something feels off to me, but I can't put my finger on what." He could practically taste the malice in the air. It was the same sort of premonition he'd had when doing patrol. The certain expectancy of an ambush, of a roadside bomb. They'd known it was there, whether they could see it or not.

Tanner nodded and sent him a shrewd look. "I'm getting the same vibe," he said. "Like there's a secondary element that we're missing."

"Exactly," Seth told him. "I've been through the file half-a-dozen times since yesterday, have practically memorized the information we have on everyone, hoping that something will jump out at me." He shook his head. "So far, nothing."

"We'll catch it," Tanner said. "I'll run first circuit and let you know how it goes." He jerked his head toward

Penelope and his lips twitched with poorly disguised humor. "How's it going with your girlfriend?"

"We're in love," Seth said in a deadpan voice, taking an instant liking to his new colleague. "She's looking at china patterns and I'm sizing my ankle for a ball and chain."

Tanner chuckled. "She looks easy enough to drag around. She's cooperating, then?"

"Fully," he told him.

"Good. That'll make your job easier."

He didn't know about that, Seth thought. But rather than comment, he merely grunted. It would have made his job easier…if he hadn't taken an immediate interest in her. If he hadn't been studying every nuance of her character since meeting her last night, from the way she cocked her head when she was thinking about something, to the backward way she stirred her tea. Counter-clockwise. Who did that? It also would have been easier if he hadn't found his loins consigned to the fiery hell of the damned every time he watched her absently lick her lips or smile or…hell, *breathe* for that matter.

Clearly he should have taken the time to get laid before embarking on this first assignment, Seth thought, giving himself a mental shake.

Intuition told him it wouldn't have mattered. He'd have still wanted her.

Because he'd been entirely too interested in what would happen when he touched her, under the guise of going into character, Seth had taken her hand as soon as they'd gotten out of the car. He'd been breathing the same air with her for several hours, had been studying every inch of exposed flesh, had been watching the way her mouth moved when she spoke and had been utterly enchanted with her.

He'd rationalized this behavior by telling himself that it was important that he knew who she was, what made her tick, what made her *her*, so that he could better play his part. So he wouldn't bungle this mission up right out of the gate because he wasn't properly prepared for his role.

He didn't know what he expected to happen when he touched her, but the burst of warmth, breathlessness and tingly sensation that followed certainly hadn't been it. The hair on his arms had stood on end and he'd felt that seemingly innocuous contact all the way down to the soles of his feet.

Bizarre. Unsettling.

He'd probably have a heart attack if he bedded her, Seth thought, shooting a look in her direction. His gaze drifted over her face and settled on her mouth, particularly the plumper lower lip. He went painfully hard again.

He made a mental note to pick up a bottle of aspirin—better safe than sorry—and while he was thinking about preventive measures, he imagined a box of condoms wouldn't be remiss, either.

Because before the weekend was out, they were going to need them.

6

CERTAIN THAT she'd put off the inevitable for as long as possible, Penelope started toward Seth, who was standing just outside of the tent. Seemingly aware that she'd moved, he turned to look at her. The instant that dark green gaze connected with hers, her heart gave a jolt and warmth puddled in her belly.

Even though she knew an unattractive man wouldn't have made for a believable "boyfriend," she almost wished Seth had been a "dog-pointer" as he'd so eloquently put it. The fact that he was six-and-a-half feet of pure masculine beauty—the worst kind of temptation—made her all too aware of him, and it was that attraction that made her all the more aware of certain parts of her own anatomy.

Parts she'd like to feel all over him, preferably naked, if she were completely honest.

Wondering when she'd become so shallow, Pen pasted a smile onto her face and bravely continued on. "I'm ready to wrap up for the day," she said. She lowered her voice. "How's everything going?"

"Nothing new to report," he said, slinging an arm over her shoulder. She repressed a full-body shiver and resisted the urge to melt into him. "The rest of the team is staying on the island and we're going to take turns running surveillance."

"Is there anything I can do to help?"

"You could start by looking up at me like you adore me. You're supposed to be my girlfriend, after all."

She chuckled and did as he asked. "Is that what your other girlfriends have done? Adored you? Worshipped the ground you walked on? Tattooed your name across their lower backs? Tramp-stamping their eternal devotion?"

He grinned. "I don't expect you to get a tattoo," he said with a humble nod. "But if you wanted to build a spectacular shrine in my honor, then I'd be cool with that."

Penelope laughed and, smiling, continued to stare up at him. She didn't have a choice. He was at least a foot taller than she was. For whatever reason, she found that especially thrilling. "A spectacular shrine? Is that all you expect of me?" She chuckled again. "Lucky me. I'll, uh… I'll get right on that."

"See that you do," he said with a grave nod. "I don't know how we'll be able to convince everyone that we're an item if you don't." He placed a mouthwateringly large hand over his heart. "I need to feel the love if I'm going to completely get into character."

He was doing a pretty damned fine job of getting into character if you asked her. He certainly didn't have any problem touching her, that was for sure. In fact, if she wasn't careful, she'd be in more danger of actually believing the ruse.

And that would be utterly disastrous. Stupidity and self-destruction in their most basic forms.

"Penelope!"

Pen turned and saw Nella's maid of honor—another former sorority sister—Patrice Anderson, hurrying toward her. Evidently Patrice had arrived early, as moral support for Nella she supposed. Pen absently wondered where Patrice was staying. She wasn't sure there was room left in the house.

"Patrice," Pen returned, giving her a small hug.

"I've only just arrived," Patrice said, sliding a covert look at Seth. Tall and willowy with exotic gray eyes and long brown hair, Patrice had always been unfairly pretty. Strangely, Pen had never hated her for it until right now. "I was able to get away a day early and wanted to see if I could do anything to help," she said.

Patrice was one of Nella's closest friends so this made perfect sense, and yet something about it felt odd to her. Evidently sensing that as well, Seth moved closer to her and seemed to be watching the exchange with more interest. The fact that he could pick up on the subtle shift in her mood when she knew she hadn't betrayed a hint of her unease made her equally unnerved and delighted.

"Not that I can think of," Pen told her. "I'm sure Nella will be glad that you're here."

Patrice looked back over her shoulder. "I haven't gone into the house yet," she said. "I saw the two of you—" once again her gaze drifted annoyingly to Seth "—and I wanted to come down and say hi." She nodded in Seth's direction. "I'm Patrice Anderson."

"Seth McCutcheon, Pen's significant other," he said, giving Penelope a gentle squeeze. His scorching gaze slid over her face with fondness and Pen felt a warm blush scald her cheeks.

Clearly he'd missed his calling—he could surely find a home on the stage.

"You're the maid of honor, right?" he said to Patrice, then looked down at Penelope. "Another of your sorority sisters? I'm glad that I'm getting to meet so many of your friends."

Patrice's gaze bounced between the two of them and her grin grew wider. "It's so nice to meet you, Seth. So how long have the two of you been dating?" Pen's short-lived romances were well-known. No doubt Patrice was asking so that she could determine the expiration date and see when Seth would be officially back on the market.

"Four months," Pen told her, smiling tightly.

Patrice's eyebrows winged up her forehead. "Four months?" she repeated. "Wow, Pen. That's a bit of a record for you, isn't it?" She glanced at Seth again and rocked back on her heels. "You must be quite special."

Seth merely chuckled and tried to look humble. "I like to think so."

"He is," Pen confirmed with an awkward nod.

"So how did the two of you meet?" Patrice asked.

"Now that's a funny story," Seth told her, shooting a look at Pen. "Why don't you tell her, baby. You're so much better at it than I am," he demurred.

The wicked twinkle in those dark green eyes told her he not only sensed her discomfort, but was enjoying it, as well. Wretch. "Er…okay." She glanced at Patrice, to find her waiting patiently. "It's quite heroic, actually," Pen told her. "He helped rescue my puppy from a storm drain."

Patrice clasped her hands to her chest and gazed at Seth as if he was a saint. "Aww," she said. "That's wonderful. So you're a fireman?"

"I am," Seth lied smoothly, to her immense shock. Just as well, though, Pen decided. In her quest to outline their relationship, she'd completely forgotten to come up with an alternate line of employment.

"Done any calendars?" Patrice quipped, flirting outrageously right in front of her.

"No," he said, laughing softly. "I—"

"He's actually going to do some boudoir photos for me while we're down here, aren't you, darling?"

His smile froze.

Pen put her hand on his chest and leaned toward Patrice as though she were sharing an intimate secret. "They're an early birthday present for me," she said. "The wedding photographer is a friend of mine and she's going to take a few shots down at the beach." She smiled up at him. "Don't worry, honey. I have every intention of applying the oil myself."

Patrice whooped and gave Pen a you-sly-dog look. "When is that particular photo shoot?" she asked.

"Not until after the wedding," Pen said, savoring a wicked thrill. She could improvise, too. "We're staying on for a couple of days. We'll stroll the beach, eat too much seafood, that sort of thing."

"I'm envious," Patrice told them. "I'll have to get on the road as soon as the ceremony is over. Mom's sixtieth birthday is on Sunday," she confided. "But it sounds like the two of you will have a wonderful time."

"Better than I imagined," Seth muttered. Pen gave him a little jab with her elbow.

"It's good to see you, Patrice," Pen said, hoping the woman would take the hint and leave before this became any more uncomfortable.

"You too." She turned to go. "Let me know if you can put me to work, Pen. I'll pitch in wherever I'm needed."

"Thanks." She breathed a silent sigh of relief as Patrice finally made her way to the house and then turned to face Seth. She chewed the inside of both cheeks—she was saving her tongue—before trusting herself to speak.

"You're a fireman? When were you planning on letting me in on that little tidbit?"

"What was I supposed to say when she asked?" His lips twisted with droll humor. "You left that out of our 'history' and I couldn't very well tell her the truth, could I?"

She supposed not. Still, she had a horrible suspicion that he was going to be dropping these little bombs on her the rest of the weekend and she was going to be powerless to keep him from doing it. One explosion after the other.

"Furthermore, I can't believe you have the nerve to

complain after your little 'boudoir photos' revelation." He chuckled low. "That was devious," he said, and to her pleased astonishment, he looked impressed.

She hadn't liked the way Patrice had been looking at him. Initially it had been quite flattering. He was pretending to be her boyfriend, after all, so she could claim temporary ownership. But even after Pen had made it clear that Seth was hers, Patrice hadn't backed off. Instead, she'd stared at Seth as though he were the last ham on the shelf on Christmas Eve.

It irritated the hell out of her.

How had this happened? Pen wondered. Had she simply been a serial dater so long that no one thought anything about making a play for a guy she was involved with because they knew he'd be history soon enough? And if so, how was she going to change that perception, particularly when she had no intention of changing her modus operandi?

Better still, why was she worried about this with a fake boyfriend? One she wasn't even really dating? Good grief, she was losing her mind. And, irrationally, she thought it was his fault.

Unfortunately, she couldn't argue with her feelings. Patrice's drooling over her guy, real or not, had supremely ticked her off. Patrice had thought he was genuinely hers, but that hadn't kept her from blatantly flirting with him right in front of her.

Clearly they were going to have to work on their performance.

And, more specifically, she was going to have to post a No Fishing sign.

"WHY FOUR MONTHS?"

Seemingly preoccupied with some thoughts that were making her forehead wrinkle, Penelope blinked and looked up at him. "What?"

"Why four months?" He'd noticed it in the file of their fake relationship. At the time, he'd thought it was an odd choice for the amount of time they'd been dating, but he'd forgotten to ask her about its significance. Given Patrice's wide-eyed astonishment when Pen had told her, there was obviously something else to it.

"Nella made sure that Trent's staff outfitted the guesthouse with a few groceries for us," she said, dodging the question altogether. She turned and started in that direction, leaving him no choice but to follow. "I'm not a gourmet chef by any stretch of the imagination, but I can probably knock up something decent. Are you hungry?"

"Yes, but that's not what I asked you," he persisted. "Why four months? What's the significance?"

"Who said it was significant?"

"Nobody had to," he said, reaching out and taking her hand. "We're supposed to be a couple, remember? Come on, Penelope. I'm not going to let it go."

She heaved an exasperated sigh and seemed to be inspecting the ground for a hole she could conveniently fall into. "Because I have a three-month rule."

"A three-month rule?"

"Yes," she admitted reluctantly. "I don't date a man beyond ninety days. Anyone who knows me well, knows that. In college, it became the source of endless entertainment and betting. I had to tell her I'd been seeing you for at least four months in order to let her, or anyone else who would know better, see that it's serious. Otherwise I wouldn't have brought you along with me, see? I've never brought anyone with me to a wedding before," she said, as though the idea were so far out of the realm of possibility, it might as well be nonexistent. She suddenly stopped and looked up at him. "Why does this matter?" she asked, exasperated. "Why do you care?"

"If we were dating in real life and I'd surpassed your ninety-day cutoff, would I know why? Would you tell me that I was special?"

She opened her mouth, closed it, then ultimately released a defeated sigh. "I suppose," she admitted grudgingly.

"*That's* why I need to know. You've given me lots of little insignificant tidbits, like your favorite color, your favorite movie, the one book you'd have to have if you were stranded on a desert island—*Pride and Prejudice*. But you've left out all the important stuff, the things that make you tick. You've given me trivia, but nothing significant."

"I've given you a hell of a lot more than you've given me," she said, arching a pointed brow.

Oh, hell, Seth thought. This wasn't going exactly the way he'd planned. Why ninety days exactly? He'd wanted to continue to grill her about her ninety-day rule and find out what had put that pucker in the middle of her forehead a minute ago. He wanted to know what had given her pause when Patrice had unexpectedly shown up. It had been a subtle shift, just the slightest tension in her small frame, but he'd caught it.

"Are you telling me that you never date anyone longer than three months, that even if it's going great and every aspect of the relationship is firing on all four cylinders, you break it off? You let the relationship *expire?*"

He didn't know why this was so important for him to understand, but he couldn't seem to keep from pressing her about it. He *had* to know how she ticked, what made her do the things she did. Should it matter? No. Was it really as relevant to what they were doing as he was making out? Also no. But that didn't change the fact that he desperately wanted to understand her. To know her. In less than twenty-four hours, this had gone beyond mere intrigue, fascination or interest. He wasn't sure he could label it at all, but if he had to try, "obsessed" probably came closer to the mark than anything else.

Penelope inserted the key into the lock and pushed open the door. Long black curly tendrils escaped her ponytail and clung to the back of her swanlike neck and he was suddenly hit with the insane urge to sweep them aside and press a kiss against her nape and breathe her in.

He was losing his damned mind, Seth decided.

She continued on into the house—he noted lots of blues, reds, and white beadboard—and set her clipboard on the bar. With a reluctant sigh, she turned to face him.

"Look, Seth, my reasons for staying single are my own. And, quite frankly, they aren't any of your business. You know what you need to know."

True, he supposed, however unpalatable. He blew out a breath and nodded.

Seemingly satisfied that the subject was closed, she relaxed enough for her shoulders to sag. "So," she said, glancing determinedly toward the kitchen. "Dinner."

Seth merely smiled. He wasn't the only one who preferred to have a purpose, he thought, following her into the kitchen. She was peering into the fridge, a thoughtful look upon her increasingly interesting face. "Hmm," she murmured. "How do you feel about a dressed-up hot ham and cheese?"

"Sounds good," Seth said. "What can I do to help?"

She nodded toward the wine refrigerator. "You can start by pouring me a glass of whatever you're having."

He chuckled and took a couple of glasses down from the rack, then inspected the various bottles. He finally settled on a nice chardonnay. "Here," he said, handing her a glass. She stopped slicing sweet peppers and onions long enough to take a grateful sip.

"Ah," she said, a slow smile spreading across her ripe lips. "Better already."

"Should I see about getting you a flask?" he teased.

She grimaced and set back to work. "I might need one by the time this weekend is over."

Working with him was that stressful, was it? He didn't know whether to be annoyed or pleased. He watched her drizzle some olive oil into a pan and dump the vegetables in. Dressed-up ham and cheese, indeed, Seth thought as she buttered four slices of Texas toast and piled them high with thick-cut ham and a couple of different kinds of cheeses. When the veggies were done, she added those as well, then transferred the sandwiches back into the pan for toasting.

Rather than stand there and watch her work, he pulled plates down from the cabinets, snagged some cutlery and set the table. He'd just finished adding pita chips to each of their plates when she made her way over. She'd halved the sandwiches and had only kept one wedge for herself.

"You didn't have to share," he said. "One would have been plenty for me."

"You're a big guy," she said, her gaze quickly skimming over him. The tops of her ears turned pink. "And I'm a little woman and want to keep it that way." She grinned at him. "Eat up."

He did and hummed with pleasure. "This is delicious. Thank you."

She popped a chip into her mouth and appeared pleased. "You're welcome. Though I'm not as good at it as I'd like to be, I enjoy cooking. One of my stepmothers had a little diner and she'd let me play around in the kitchen. I learned a lot from her."

Another stepparent, Seth thought. How many had she had? he wondered. But after her recent none-of-your-business comment, he had no intention of asking her.

He could ask her something else though.

"So what's the deal with Patrice?"

She took a sip of wine and her gaze tangled with his. "What do you mean?"

"You tensed up when you were talking to her. Was that because we were officially 'on' or because something about her arriving early rang an alarm bell?"

"Both, actually, but more so the latter." She frowned thoughtfully. "It's not like Patrice to be on time for anything, much less early," she said. "I don't know if this whole situation is making me paranoid or what. It just struck me as a little odd."

Patrice obviously hadn't called ahead to let Pen know that she was coming. "Do you think Nella knew she was on her way down?"

She hesitated. "I don't think so," she said. "That wasn't the impression I'd gotten. And Nella didn't say a word when I was talking to her." She shrugged. "Then again, maybe it's not a big deal. Nella's had a lot on her mind and if Patrice is here to help lighten her load, then that's wonderful. I'm probably just pissed because she was flirting with you," she admitted, to his astonishment.

"You think?"

"Probably." She nodded. "It's bad form to flirt with your friend's guy, especially when she knows that you're special."

He couldn't help the grin that spread across his lips and laughed out loud when she looked up, an expression of mortified horror on her face. "I'm special, am I?"

"You know what I mean," she said, taking another drink of wine. "I'm talking about that three-month rule."

Rather than needle her any more, he reluctantly turned the conversation back to business. "So did you notice anything bizarre today? Anything strike you as odd?"

"No," she said. "Though it was the day from hell.

Evidently our caterer was under the impression that we'd canceled our entire order, which would have been a disaster of epic proportions. And when I called to confirm the rehearsal time with the pastor who is marrying Trent and Nella, he seemed completely baffled. Evidently he'd been told the service had been moved to Sunday."

Seth's antennae twitched. "By whom?"

She shrugged. "I don't know and neither does he. His secretary took the call."

"Has anything like this ever happened before?"

She looked offended. "To me? No," she said. "I don't just double-check—I quadruple-check," she told him. "People make mistakes all the time and the wrong stroke of a key when confirming a time for the food, the pastor, the band, anything…can ruin a wedding. I—" She stopped and her eyes widened. "This isn't a coincidence, is it?" she asked, turning a bit green.

He didn't think so. "Probably not," Seth said. "Who would have access to these details, the caterer being used, the person officiating at the ceremony?"

"The usual suspects," Pen told him. "Anyone close to Trent and Nella. Any member of the wedding party."

"And members of your staff," he added.

"No," she said flatly. "I trust each one of them implicitly. Furthermore, Monica is the only one who has been brought up to speed on stuff."

She could trust them all she wanted to, but it was his job not to trust anybody. And right now, with the exception of her, everyone was a suspect. Canceling the food and trying to put off the pastor were simple attempts at stopping the wedding, but they spelled trouble. Those attempts took guts because the person behind them ran the risk of getting caught, being remembered. It was amateurish, yes, but it was also reckless. And a reckless person could be dangerous.

As for Trent and Nella, he'd met with the couple earlier and had been extremely impressed with both of them. He'd been following Trent's career for years and was unbelievably pleased with the man's down-to-earth attitude. Nella quite obviously adored him and Seth had gotten the overwhelming impression that the sentiment was returned. No wonder Pen had rated them a nine, Seth thought. Hell, he would have given them a ten.

"Would Patrice have any reason to want to sabotage the wedding? Any grudge?" he asked, wondering again about her interesting timing.

Penelope shook her head. "None that I can think of. She squealed along with the rest of us when Nella told us about the proposal. She hosted a wedding shower and even tried to throw the bachelorette party, only Nella didn't want one," she confided. "Overall, she seems to be quite happy for her." She paused, as if searching her memory. "Patrice is a bit of a prophet of doom. Her marriage only lasted a few months, so she's not exactly enamored with the institution."

"She's divorced?"

She nodded.

"Did you plan her wedding, as well?"

Another small nod. "Yes," she said on a sigh.

"What happened?"

"Affair."

"Guilty party?"

"Him."

Seth winced. He'd only just met Patrice and could imagine how well that had gone over. Honestly, why bother? Why say *I do* when you know *you won't?* "So she'd have reason to want to save her friend the same kind of heartache. Would she do that? Would that be enough?"

"I don't know," Pen admitted. "She and Nella are close, obviously. But Patrice hasn't said a negative word to me about Nella tying the knot."

"How long has it been?"

"Since Patrice's wedding?"

"Yeah."

"It was a Christmas wedding," she said. "So around eighteen months."

Seth mulled that over. "We definitely need to keep an eye on her," he told her. "From what you've observed, it's out of character for her to arrive early and she has more than enough reason to think marriage on the whole is a bad idea, particularly for a good friend."

Penelope released a breath. "I suppose so."

Seth's cell phone suddenly sounded at his waist. He unclipped it from his side and checked the display. Katie. She'd worry if he didn't answer, and if he sent her to voice mail she'd just call back. He looked up at Penelope, shooting her an apologetic smile. "I need to take this."

Looking intensely curious, she merely nodded. "Sure."

He stood and backed away from the table. "Leave the dishes," he instructed her. "You cooked. I'll clean."

She made a moue of pleasure and nodded, then helped herself to another glass of wine. "That's fair," she said. "No objection from me."

That was novel, Seth thought. He wondered if the same sentiment would hold true when he kissed her. Because he fully intended to do so the instant the opportunity presented itself.

7

THOUGH SHE KNEW it was impolite to eavesdrop, there was nothing wrong with Pen's hearing. And since Seth had only moved into the living room, she couldn't help but hear virtually every word he was saying. She'd known from the instant he'd looked at the display that this was a personal call, not business related. She'd seen the slightest upturn of his mouth, the faintest smile that made her long to know who had put it there.

Aha, Pen thought, cocking an ear toward the living room. It was someone named Katie. An irrational stab of jealousy momentarily pierced her. Of course it was a woman, she thought with a fatalistic sigh. Just because he wasn't married, that didn't mean that he was completely unattached. He could still have a girlfriend. Or maybe someone who hadn't quite made the upgrade to girlfriend status. Hell, for all she knew, this was a friend-with-benefits relationship, where they simply got together when the mood struck for a little recreational no-strings sex.

Her eye began to twitch.

"Yeah, it's beautiful down here. Very peaceful. Has Mitch ever been to the beach?"

Mitch? Who was Mitch?

"We need to plan a trip this summer. Bring him down and let him play in the sand." He chuckled. "He'd love it. Yeah, sure. It'd be great. Maybe come down in October when the bulk of the tourists more or less clear out and the kids are back in school."

So he was planning a vacation with this Katie person and her child? A young child by the sounds of it. Her eyes widened. Could it be *his* child? she wondered and gasped. Was Katie his baby mama?

She tossed back the rest of her wine.

He laughed again and a smile entered his voice. "Yeah, I hear him. Put the little rug rat on the phone." Another pause, then, "Hey, buddy. Are you being good for mama? You are? Good. What was that? You want to ride in my truck? Sure, bud. I'll take you for a spin when I get back, okay? Okay," he said, his voice full of fondness. "Let me talk to mama again, okay? Love you, buddy."

Aww, Pen thought. *How sweet.* She didn't know for sure who this little boy was, but he was lucky that Seth was in his life.

"Yeah, he told me," he said. "I told him I'd take him for a ride again when I got back." He laughed, the sound soft and slightly rough. "Hey, I can make anything look cool, little sister. Even a car seat."

Little sister?

"You know it," he laughed. "Right. I'll talk to ya'll tomorrow, sis. Love you, too. Bye."

Seth walked back into the kitchen and held up his phone. "My sister," he explained with a sheepish smile.

"I heard, sorry. I wasn't trying to listen, but…" She shrugged. "And a nephew?"

He nodded and started clearing the table. "Mitchell. He's two and half. Adorable."

"They typically are at that age," she said. "They call them the terrible twos, but in my experience it's not until they hit around three to three and a half that the true tantrums set in."

He filled the sink with soapy water. "Your experience? You've got nieces and nephews?"

"Oodles of them," she sighed, feeling warm and pleasant from the alcohol currently moving through her system. Honestly, with all her half siblings combined, they could have their own football team. There were some she was closer to than others, some that she'd bonded with and continued to keep in touch with after their parents had broken things off. Her family tree was mangled all to hell and back, Pen thought with an inward snort. She only had one true sibling, her younger sister Phoebe, who was currently in England on a student exchange program. As an English Lit major, nothing could have been more fitting. She got the occasional postcard rhapsodizing clotted cream and scones and bemoaning the lack of ice in her drinks, but overall she knew her sister was having the time of her life.

As for her parents, her mother and husband number four were panning for gold in Alaska—Geoff was the quintessential mountain man—and her father, who had just recently divorced wife number five, was on a spiritual retreat in Sedona, looking for his "true" self via vortexes and a self-proclaimed shaman. Honestly, she didn't mind that either of her parents danced to the beat of their own drums, it was just remarkable to her that they both had no trouble finding someone to do that dancing with them. She'd seen them both utterly euphoric, blissfully content, mildly dissatisfied and completely miserable—all on account of love.

No, thank you. Pen didn't want any part of it, other than the business that enabled her to earn a living. The rest—the romance—she could live without. And she fully intended to. Her gaze slid to Seth, who was standing at the kitchen sink washing dishes, and her heart gave an unexpected and odd pang. Only he could make the domesticated chore look sexy. She loved the way the hair around the nape of his neck curled. Muscles rippled beneath the thin black T-shirt and she could just make out the fluted hollow of his spine. Her gaze slid lower and she felt her nipples bead behind her bra.

He had the best ass she'd ever, *ever* seen. In all honesty, she thought there was something pretty ridiculous-looking about a man's penis—not that she couldn't appreciate one when it was being properly utilized, but a bit funny all the same. But a man's ass… Now that was the money shot.

And his was priceless.

"Mitch is all I've got," Seth told her, interrupting her blatant ogling. "He kind of got the shaft in the father department, so I'm trying to make up for that as best I can."

They really needed to abandon the rescuing the puppy from the storm drain aspect of their history, Pen decided. Seth McCutcheon didn't need the artifice. He was one of those rare guys who actually did the right thing.

"I'm sure your sister appreciates that."

He dried a plate and put it away. "She does. It hasn't been easy for her, I know."

Was that the reason he came out of the military? Pen wondered. Had he promised his sister that he would? He hadn't said a word about his own parents and she couldn't think of a reason to ask without it coming off as prying. Which is exactly what it would be. But the more he revealed about himself, the more he was going to expect of her. And her parents and their marathon of marriages wasn't a topic she wished to discuss with him or anyone else for that matter.

Moving methodically around the kitchen, he quickly wiped everything down, then rinsed out the sink. When he pulled a broom and dustpan from the pantry and proceeded to sweep the kitchen floor, she found herself smiling.

He caught her. "Is something funny?"

"Not at all," she said. "I'm just amazed at your thoroughness, that's all." She'd be willing to bet every one of his coat hangers were the same color, shape and size and were properly spaced on the closet rod. She'd noticed that he'd been tidy at his new apartment, but had wondered if that was the case only because he hadn't been there long enough to make a real mess.

Evidently not.

"There's not much point in doing something if you aren't going to do it right," he said. He looked up and his gaze lingered over her breasts, up her neck, and settled long enough on her mouth to make her breathing go shallow. "Being meticulous typically pays off." His gaze met hers. "Surely given your line of work, you of all people understand that, right?"

Her mouth had gone dry and her glass was empty. Damn. She cleared her throat. "Yes, of course," she said, her voice a bit strangled.

"You need a refill?" he asked solicitously, his lips twitching.

"Nope," she said, standing up. "I've had two glasses already and that's my limit." Any more and she'd be in danger of losing her self-control or common sense, both of which seemed to be in short supply whenever she was within a few feet of him.

He nodded, then glanced at the clock on the microwave. "I need to take a walk around the property," he said. "Why don't you come with me?"

"I think I'd better stay here." She needed some much needed distance and knew she wasn't going to be getting any of that over the next couple of days.

"It's going to look like I'm skulking around if I'm alone. Whereas if you were with me, it would look like we were taking a romantic evening stroll."

That made perfect sense and yet she was getting the distinct impression that she was being manipulated, that he actually wanted her company. Dangerous, Pen thought. She should stay right here, take a cold shower and count the many reasons why genuinely liking Seth was a bad idea. She should and yet…

"Skulking," she remarked. "Now there's a word you don't often hear."

"Do you need a definition?" he asked, shooting her an innocent look.

She smirked. "No, smart-ass, I do not."

A surprised laugh rumbled up his throat as they got ready to leave. "Are you sure you won't have another glass of wine? I think your tongue needs loosening up a little bit more."

Any more wine and it would come unhinged altogether. He fell in behind her and then, ever the gentleman, reached around her and opened the door. A soft breeze blew in off the water, lifting her hair. Half the sun had dipped below the horizon, painting the sky and water in beautiful warm tones, a few pinks and purples thrown in for good measure.

Though she'd expected it, the feel of his big hand finding hers was still a bit of a lovely shock. "Keeping up appearances," he said, giving her fingers a slight squeeze.

Right, Penelope thought, releasing a slow breath.

"Where exactly are we going?"

"We're just going to walk along the perimeter of Trent's estate."

"To make sure nobody's lurking in the bushes?"

He was scanning the area, doing an admirable job of make the intense scrutiny look casual. She knew better, of course. Had she asked him, she knew he could tell her exactly how many blooms were on the bushes close to the house and which shades were drawn on the windows and which weren't. He didn't miss a trick, she was certain. "Something like that."

"What would you do if you actually found someone?"

"Whatever's necessary."

That covered a lot of ground, Pen thought, as goose bumps skittered over her skin.

"Don't look, but someone's watching from the window in the cupola."

Even though he'd told her not to look, her head inexplicably turned in that direction. Then to her immense surprise, which instantly turned to delight, he caught it with his mouth.

There was something to be said for a man who was naturally thorough, Pen thought dizzily as her hand landed on his chest and fisted in his shirt. Her entire body felt as if it had been doused in gasoline and then set ablaze. She savored the burn, reveled in it even as her insides melted and her blood scorched through her veins.

His lips were warm and soft and firm and moved over hers with a lazy purposefulness that told her that kissing wasn't merely the appetizer before the main course. He obviously enjoyed the taste of her, the feel of her against his mouth.

Though she knew he was merely doing this as a preventive measure that he'd improvised to keep her from blowing their cover, she nevertheless could appreciate his expertise…and he was definitely an expert. Last night's kamikaze kiss had been nothing compared to this slow exploration of her mouth. Still, she wasn't sure which one she like better—they both left her breathless.

He groaned low in his throat, the sound reverberating off her own tongue and dragged her closer to him, fitting her body more closely to his. He was big and warm and wonderful and she loved the way her own body felt when it was next to his—enervated, alive and on fire. Like she was plugged into his energy, was feeding off of it. She needed it, craved it….

And that was the danger, Pen realized foggily, as his tongue tangled skillfully around hers. She couldn't afford to need anyone…least of all a pretend boyfriend she suspected could do the one thing no other guy had ever managed.

He could steal her heart.

And then he'd have the power to break it.

SETH KNEW he was taking extreme liberties with his stealth kiss, but hadn't been able to resist the opportunity. He'd told her not to look, knowing that she'd try, and had easily captured her mouth under the guise of maintaining their cover.

He was a self-serving opportunistic bastard, Seth thought, molding her small womanly body closer to his, and he'd never been less ashamed of himself. Who had time to feel remorse—who would even bother?—when she felt like this against him? When she tasted like wine and cheese, and her mouth was plum soft and juicy and her sweet body was pressed so closely against his own.

He'd tasted her startled breath, then the following

sigh. Even though he'd suspected that she'd wanted it as much as he had, savoring those two things against his tongue were all the proof he needed that the desire was mutual.

Seth McCutcheon had been stealing kisses since kindergarten. He regularly found third base in junior high and lost his virginity to an *older woman,* a sophomore, the summer before his freshman year of high school. He knew when a girl was into him. He recognized the tells—the fluttering heartbeat at the base of the throat, the sidelong glances, the lingering attention on his ass. Gratifyingly Pen, in particular, seemed to like his ass. He could read the body language, the certain way a woman cocked her head, the unconscious lean in, the unwitting need to get closer, to breathe and smell a person in.

He'd watched Penelope's eyes widen and darken last night when she'd unexpectedly dropped by his place. He'd recognized that instant flash of awareness, because he'd felt it himself and known that they were going to be in serious trouble.

While Seth was aware that he was only supposed to be pretending that he and Penelope were an item, and he further suspected that he wasn't supposed to allow, much less encourage, things to go beyond simple playacting, he couldn't seem to help himself. She obliterated his self-control, beckoned his wilder tendencies.

Though he could think of at least half-a-dozen reasons off the top of his head why they shouldn't do this—the most significant being that he imagined Ranger Security would disapprove—he knew he wasn't going to heed a single one of them.

He wanted her.

And from the tension and desperation in her touch, she wanted him as well.

He had a feeling his bogus fling was going to be anything but fake. Something about that unexplainable premonition gave him the briefest pause, made the nape of his neck tingle with…expectation?

With difficulty, he reluctantly ended the kiss. Pen's lashes fluttered and she looked up at him, still seemingly dazed. Something in his chest shifted and he smiled down at her. "I thought I told you not to look."

She blinked and drew back, a faint blush coloring her cheeks. "Sorry," she murmured.

He took her hand once more, noting the shadow in the window was still there. Trent's sister, he thought, but couldn't be sure. Furthermore, Paul, who was part of Pen's crew, was having an evening smoke down by the pier and seemed to be looking up at the house. He noticed Seth and lifted his hand in a casual wave.

A droll smile slid over her lips. "You just played me, didn't you?"

"Sorry?"

She jabbed him with her elbow, shook her head and laughed. "No you're not," she said. "Well done, Mr. McCutcheon." She faked a couple of coughs and lifted her hand to her mouth, pretended to spit something into her palm and toss it on the ground.

He frowned down at her. "Are you all right?"

"Fine," she said. "Just trying to hack up that hook, line and sinker."

Seth felt a laugh break up in his throat. "I didn't plan it exactly," he lied. "But I will admit to taking unfair advantage. And I'll also admit I'm not sorry." He paused. "You?"

The crash of the surf and night sounds settled around them and the wind was warm and easy. "Nah," she said. "I'm only sorry I enjoyed it as much as I did."

He chuckled again, surprised at her honesty. "That's a hell of a thing to be sorry about," he said. "But it's a compliment...I think."

"It is," she confirmed, then merely shrugged. "But it's a bad idea."

They were talking bigger picture here, not just the kiss, and he knew it. "Probably," he agreed. "But I have to admit I like it."

She inclined her head. "Then I'll take that as a compliment."

"It's definitely intended to be one. You're a good kisser," he remarked. "If you were trying to discourage me, you should have botched it," he told her, shooting her a smile. "Remember that next time."

He felt her laugh before he heard it. "Next time?"

"It could happen again." In fact, he fully intended to make sure that it did. Stupid? Reckless? Foolhardy? Yes, yes and yes, but unavoidable all the same. Seth wasn't in the habit of lying, least of all to himself. What was the point? He could go through a laundry list of reasons why he shouldn't make a play for Penelope Hart, but ultimately none of those reasons was going to matter.

He wanted her. She wanted him.

In fact, in so many ways, she was the perfect woman. She wasn't looking for a long-term commitment—was actively avoiding it, in fact—and wouldn't expect a declaration of love or any of the other sticky wickets that generally came up when dealing with the fairer sex. They could engage in a little mutually satisfying phenomenal sex, and given the way his dick was trying to come out of his shorts, he knew the sex would be better than spectacular. Then they could part as friends, both of them satisfied and happy.

Win, win.

And if he was simplifying this a little too much or was mildly certain that it wouldn't go off completely the way he was envisioning it, then he was going to ignore those thoughts altogether and pretend he wasn't having them. He knew he'd have to deal with the consequences of these actions at some point, but by the time that inevitability rolled around, he would have already gotten what he wanted.

Her.

"You're awfully quiet," he remarked, intrigued by what her continued silence meant. Like him, was she ready to say to hell with everything and go for it? Or was she trying to figure out a way to get him to back off, to keep things on the level they were supposed to be playing?

"Who was looking out the window?" she asked. Or maybe she wasn't thinking about him at all, Seth realized, the thought pricking his ego.

"I'm not sure, but I think it was Trent's sister."

"Lucy?" She hummed thoughtfully under her breath. "She's a sweet girl," Pen said. "I think she's really looking forward to having Nella in the family. Their mother can be a bit…stern," she said, taking the diplomatic approach.

"Is that code for a real bitch?"

She smiled at him. "I would never say that."

"But you'd think it," he said, laughing. "So you don't think Lucy could be behind this?"

She paused, seeming to be giving his question serious thought before answering. "I really don't," she said. "But honestly it's hard for me to imagine any of the women who are here deliberately trying to sabotage Trent and Nella's wedding."

Be that as it may, the fact remained that it was most likely a woman making the threats, definitely someone who was close enough to receive the necessary invitations, and there were only so many women in Trent's circle. That significantly narrowed the pool of suspects, if you asked Seth.

Improbable or not, someone they trusted was behind this. And that made that person all the more dangerous. But the same instincts that told him there was a missing element here also told him that he could handle it, that he would succeed. Arrogance? No. Arrogance could get you killed.

Confidence, on the other hand, was invaluable.

His gaze slid to Pen, who seemed to be deep in thought. Probably second-guessing her staff, he imagined, since it would be been extremely easy for someone in her circle to cancel the caterer and attempt to postpone the pastor. Then again, why would they bother, knowing how manically prepared she was? Knowing that she'd catch it? No matter how he tried to put it all together, the pieces didn't fit. But he had every intention of making sure they did before the weekend was out.

In the meantime, they had the rest of the night to get through…and he was hoping they were going to get to work on authenticating their performance a little more.

Preferably in bed.

8

"OKAY, WHAT HAPPENED?" Monica demanded first thing the next morning.

Pen feigned interest in watching the rental company unload the chairs. "I don't know what you mean."

"Yes, you do. Someone said they saw you and Mr. Gorgeous in a lip-lock last night and that was in *plain view*. I want to know what happened behind closed doors."

Someone saw them, huh? She knew exactly who'd seen them—Paul, she was sure. Her official heavy lifter was smirking at her when they'd made the return circuit to the guesthouse. She knew exactly what had put that knowing smile on Paul's face and congratulated herself for further perpetuating the idea that they were really a couple.

Despite the fact that Paul didn't think Seth was her type, she knew she had him fooled, at least. No doubt he'd been catching a smoke before going out with the others, she thought and made a mental note to make sure that he hadn't left any unsightly cigarette butts behind.

He typically didn't, but she liked to be certain. She never wanted to give any of her clients a reason to complain. Being courteous was just as important as orchestrating the perfect wedding.

As for what had happened behind closed doors… Pen's cheeks puffed as she exhaled mightily.

Absolutely nothing.

She'd cited being tired and having a lot to do the next morning. Then she'd made some sort of awkward gesture with her thumb and hastily retreated to her bedroom. Thankfully, both guest rooms had been outfitted with en suite facilities and she'd run herself a bubble bath and tried not to think about the six-and-a-half feet of masculine temptation that would be literally ready for action if she so much as crooked her finger.

It had been hard.

And he'd been hard, too, when they'd been kissing, so she knew exactly what she was missing.

Oy.

Suffice it to say that Seth McCutcheon was an extremely large man and, given the way a certain part of him had been nudging high on her belly, the rest of him was definitely proportionate.

Her mouth watered anew, her breasts tingled and a hot snake of heat coiled low in her belly, making her resist the urge to squirm. She felt she'd been resisting that urge for a damned eternity instead of a mere twenty-four hours, and didn't have any idea how on earth she was going to hold out for another night.

"Why are you turning red?" Monica demanded, her voice full of insinuation. "If nothing happened, then why do you look like you let Raggedy Ann apply your blush?"

"Because it's hotter than four hundred hells out here," Pen complained good-naturedly, which was the truth.

Though she would never admit it to Nella, she had to agree with Lucy when it came to the whole issue of holding the wedding outside. Early morning would have offered the best temperature, but who held a wedding at seven in the morning? Two o'clock was the norm and two o'clock here, particularly beneath the tents containing the food and dance floor, would be utterly stifling.

As such, they'd opted for an evening wedding. The festivities would begin at seven o'clock, the actual service over by seven-thirty, and then the cooler evening breezes would keep the icing from melting off the cake and the dancers from expiring in the heat.

Provided everyone lived through it, which was where Seth and his team came in. He'd been floating around today helping out as needed and seemed to be paying particular attention to the women around the house. She knew Seth wasn't flirting, which would be bad form considering he was supposed to be here as her boyfriend, but had been chatting with them all quite a bit. Even Monica, who thankfully didn't realize that he'd moved her onto the official suspect list. The same held true for Patrice. But in that case, Patrice was the one who was laughing a little too loudly and standing a little too close. Gratifyingly, Seth always moved back, lengthening the distance between them.

He was faithful, her pretend boyfriend, she thought, and squashed another smile.

No doubt he would be equally faithful to a real girlfriend. Granted she hadn't known him long, but in her line of work, she could typically spot the cheaters of both the male and female varieties, and Seth just didn't seem the type. No, he was a guy who would tell a woman the truth at the end of the evening to prevent her from waiting on a call that was never going to come. He was the kind of guy who put more stock in honesty than diplomacy. He spoke his mind and didn't waste time.

Honestly, if she didn't know any better, she'd think he was perfect. Or at least as close to perfect as a man could get.

"Are you telling me nothing happened?" Monica persisted. "Absolutely nothing?"

"I'm not going to tell you anything," Pen said, counting pedestals as they came off the truck. She was supposed to have twenty, ten on each side. "Because it's none of your business."

Monica stuck her tongue out at her. "Boo hiss. You know I want details." Her gaze drifted to Seth once more. "That man is one long, tall drink of water."

Yes, Pen thought, grinding her teeth. *She knew.*

Monica blinked innocently. "You look pissed," she remarked. She studied Penelope thoughtfully for a moment, then she gasped and her eyes widened. "Wait a minute," she breathed, as though she'd just unlocked some secret compartment inside Pen's brain. "That's not pissed. That's jealous. Oh my God! You're *jealous!*" She gave a little bouncy squeal. "You don't like it when

I drool over your pretend boyfriend. Oh, oh, this is epic! This is—ow!"

"Cut it out," Pen told her, not the least bit sorry that she'd whacked her friend with her trusty clipboard. "I am not jealous," she said, enunciating every word, trying to make the lie more believable. "I'm annoyed. I've got a wedding to pull off and a crazy person doing their best to ruin it. But all you can talk about is the guy who is supposed to be making sure that nothing goes horribly, heinously wrong. Unless you've forgotten, we're talking about a potential *murder* here," she reminded Monica in her stiffest, most stuffy tone. "Death at a wedding, then, remember?" Penelope quoted. "Someone dies here, they not only lose their lives, but I lose my business. Have you thought of that? Who'd hire me after that?"

She hated that she sounded so self-serving and mercenary…but she couldn't help it. Naturally she didn't want anyone to get hurt, but she'd be a fool not to consider what would happen to her business if someone did.

She'd be ruined.

She'd have to start over in another field and she could kiss goodbye the house she wanted. Her little plot of permanence, some place of her own that she desperately needed. She'd actually taken a home buyer's guide into the tub with her last night and looked at what was currently on the market. She'd been too afraid of getting her hopes up. It was the first time she'd allowed herself the luxury. She'd found a lovely antebellum a few blocks from her shop that she'd instantly fallen in love with. It was in her price range and she could even walk to work.

It had lots of stained glass and flowers and a whimsical turret on the second story.

She'd melted when she saw it, much the same way she'd melted the first time she'd laid eyes on Seth McCutcheon.

There was a frightening insight in that, but Pen refused to excavate the emotional territory enough to unearth its meaning. Some things were better left alone. She instinctively knew this was one of them.

Monica's face fell. "Goodness," she said. "I'm sorry, Pen. I hadn't even thought... I hadn't considered..."

"It's all right, Mon. I *have* to consider. It's my business."

She grimaced. "Yeah, but if you go under, then we're all unemployed."

Pen grinned. "There is that."

"So has anything else happened?" Monica asked, thankfully onto a new topic. "Any more letters or threats?"

She didn't tell her what Seth thought of the cancellations yesterday. No need to worry her further. "Not as of yet, no."

"Do you think the person might have just been bluffing? If they're close, then they know that the wedding is going off anyway, right? They have to know that Trent and Nella haven't called anything off."

"True," Pen conceded. "But it may just mean that they're biding their time, waiting for the perfect moment to sabotage everything."

"Well, if that's the case, then they're leaving it to the last minute, aren't they?" She looked around, evidently considering everyone as a possible suspect now. "I mean, the rehearsal is tonight. Besides, they're going to have a hard time getting anything past those Ranger Security boys," she said.

Pen knew that was right. Using Trent's celebrity status as an excuse, they were ferrying guests over in vans from a nearby marina and were wanding everyone for possible weapons. Purses and bags would be searched and nothing was coming onto the island without being checked first. In addition to that precaution, Trent's regular security contingent would be circling the island in patrol boats, making sure that no one attempted to come ashore via a different route.

"Unless the person is already here," Monica murmured, her eyes narrowed shrewdly. "In which case, how will we know who is behind it? We can't very well go up and start accusing everyone, can we?"

"Seth's on it," Pen told her. "We need to leave the sleuthing to the professionals and do our dead level best to make sure that Trent and Nella's wedding goes off without a hitch. That's our job," she said to Monica, but the reminder was as much for herself as anyone.

Monica suddenly smiled. "I rather think I'd prefer to be a detective."

Pen chuckled, not the least bit surprised. "In that case why don't you hit Paul on the walkie-talkie and find out why it's taking him so long to get those runners up here?" Paul wasn't what one would call a self-starter, but did as he was told and, at the moment, he seemed to be under the delusional impression that this was a beach vacation instead of a wedding.

Monica heaved a put-upon sigh. "That wasn't exactly the kind of detecting I meant."

"But that is the kind you're getting paid for. Scoot," she shooed her. "Get moving. We've got more to do today than we can conceivably handle."

Her assistant heaved a breath. "You say that every time."

"Because it's always the truth."

Nella suddenly burst out of the house, her face white, tears streaming over her cheeks. "Pen!"

Pen's heart stopped. "Nella?"

Nella's face crumpled as she hurried toward her. "Pen, my d-dress," she sobbed. "It's ruined!"

SETH WATCHED silently as Penelope inspected Nella's gown. Trent, his mother and Patrice attempted to comfort the crying bride-to-be, while Lucy, Trent's sister, stood nearby and looked on awkwardly. She was pale, but that could be said for the rest of the women as well.

Because she knew that Seth couldn't ask any questions in front of anyone without possibly tipping their hand, Pen did her best to ask the questions he would most want to know. That she had the presence of mind to do this despite what could only be described as a potentially show-stopping disaster showed him a lot about her character.

"Nella, when were the alterations on the dress complete?"

"Last week," she sniffed. "I went in and tried it on, everything fit perfectly."

"They stored it in the bag and you took it home?"

She nodded.

"Has it been out of the bag since? Have you shown it to anyone at all?"

"I showed it to Lucy yesterday," she said.

"Did you take it out of the bag?"

"No," she said, looking thoughtful. Her gaze tangled with Pen's. "I didn't. It…it could have been like this yesterday and I wouldn't have known," she told her, seemingly horrified all over again.

That's because the damage to the dress had been done on the back, where it wouldn't have shown had she only unzipped the front of the bag and moved the plastic aside to show off the front. He and Pen shared a look. Which meant this could have been done in the store before Nella brought it home or at any time over the past week while it was still at her house. Or it could have been done here.

It really was a shame, too, Seth thought, feeling sorry for Nella. The entire back of the dress looked like someone had taken a box cutter and sliced it to ribbons. It was definitely beyond repair and he wasn't sure what would happen now. Though he had little experience with weddings, it was his understanding that, for the bride, the dress was the pièce de résistance. Furthermore, that dress had probably cost as much as a compact car and now it was utterly ruined.

Well, at least one thing was certain. Whoever was making the threats was close enough to Nella to have the time and the opportunity to destroy her dress. And that was too close for Seth's liking.

Pen inspected the back of the dress, fingered the

shredded satin. Finally, she looked up and sighed. "I don't see how this can be repaired, at least not in time for the wedding tomorrow."

Nella nodded, dabbing at her eyes.

Pen leaned over and took Nella's hand. "Nella, I know that this is heartbreaking and I can't imagine what would possess someone to do something like this to your dress," she added, her voice throbbing with anger. "This was an heirloom, something that you'd intended to preserve and pass onto your own daughter and—" She couldn't finish. "I know that this is a blow. But after the wedding, we'll find someone to fix it as best they can. It won't look exactly like the dress you'd wanted, but it will be close enough to serve its purpose."

Trent's mother spoke up for the first time. "Elise Martine can repair it, dear," she said, laying a hand on Nella's shoulder. "As Penelope says, it's not ever going to be the same dress again, but it can be salvaged."

"In the interim, we're going to have to go to Plan B," Penelope said.

"Do we have a Plan B?" Nella asked, her voice still thick with unshed tears.

Pen smiled. "We do now. You're going to have to go get another dress today," she said. "I'll make some calls, find the best boutiques and—" she nodded toward Lucy and Patrice "—you'll need a couple of pairs of eyes to make sure that you make the best choice."

Brilliant, Seth thought. No doubt she would find something else to occupy Trent's mother's time and that would free up him and his team to do a little recon through the women's things. In particular, Trent would be looking for a sharp instrument… and a red pen.

"Of course we'll help, won't we, Lucy?" Patrice chimed in. Honestly she was almost too happy. On the other end of the spectrum, Lucy looked like she'd prefer a colonic cleanse. He couldn't imagine why either one of them would have any reason to sabotage Trent and Nella like this, but common sense said that one of them was the guilty party. Evidently, Pen thought so, too.

Armed with a plan, Nella stood and turned directly into Trent's arms. "It'll be all right, sweetheart," he told her, pressing a kiss onto the top of her head. "You could wear a potato sack and I'd still think you were the most beautiful bride on the planet."

Sincerity rang so strongly in his voice that Seth didn't doubt for an instant that Trent was making a true statement. For one terrifying moment, he wondered what it would feel like to be that tied to another person, that invested. And for reasons he couldn't explain, his gaze drifted to Penelope.

Nella smiled up at Trent. "Are you thinking we should start a new tradition? The potato sack wedding dress?"

"It's got a certain cachet," he said.

She hesitated, then patted him on the arm. "I'll go see what I can find."

"I'll get the phone book," Trent's mother said, seemingly desperate to be helpful. Her mouth had formed a grim line and, when she'd seen the back of the dress, Seth had noticed that her eyes had watered with unshed tears. She looked at her son. "Trent, I'd like a word later, please."

No doubt that was going to be the what-the-hell-are-you-not-telling-me? conversation, because after this incident, she was shrewd enough to understand that something was amiss. Though he wasn't comfortable ruling anyone out completely, like Pen, he didn't think Trent's mother was behind any of this either.

Trent's mother hurried out of the room after the other three, leaving the rest of them alone. He and Trent helped Pen put the ruined dress back into the bag and then Trent looked at Seth. "It has to be someone close," he said, his voice low and sick. "Someone we trust, obviously, which makes me feel a little foolish, but…" He shrugged helplessly and gave a humorless laugh. "What can I do?" Trent asked.

"Occupy your mother," Seth told him. "Honestly, I don't think that she's involved, but while I'm in the house looking through Patrice and Lucy's things, I want to go ahead and do a thorough search so that we can completely rule her out. Also, make sure that Nella goes in her car and that the other two leave their vehicles here. You can tell them that we might need to move them or something—make up some story—but I want to sweep the cars as well."

"You think it could be one of them?" Trent asked.

"No one else has had the kind of access required to pull this off," Pen piped up. She gestured to the bag. "This wasn't done at the boutique—the owner is meticulous about inspecting everything that leaves the store. So that means this was done either at Nella's house or here. And both Lucy and Patrice have been both places."

"I don't know if Lucy has been to Nella's in the past week," Trent said, looking thoughtful.

"Check with Nella," Seth told him. "Also find out if Nella has a Hide-A-Key and who would know about it if she did."

Trent nodded and set off.

Pen and Seth shared a look. "This is bad, isn't it?" she said.

"It's bad for the dress, but it's actually not bad for the case. We've narrowed our suspects down to two and, despite what's happened to the dress, I don't think Lucy or Patrice is likely to try to kill anyone. I think the whole 'murder' aspect of the threat was for dramatic effect. They're sabotaging—being hurtful, certainly—but they aren't hurting *anybody* and that's what's important." And even if they were planning on hurting someone, Seth would make sure that he stopped them first. Something still wasn't quite right, but at least now they were on the right path. They had a direction, even if it wasn't one they'd wanted to take.

Pen chuckled grimly. "True, but Trent might hurt someone when he finds out who's behind this. Nella's gown was custom-made. She had more than eighteen months invested in it. The lace on the front was actually from her mother's wedding dress and the veil had been her grandmother's. They'd added a few things to make it coordinate with Nella's dress, but both were heirloom pieces."

"The veil was untouched?"

"Yes, thank God, though I think we should probably move it down to the guesthouse with us."

He nodded. "When is Nella's mother supposed to arrive?"

"This afternoon," Pen said. She massaged the bridge of her nose. "She'll be relieved that the front of the dress wasn't ruined."

"Was it common knowledge that the lace was from her mother's gown?"

Pen frowned, her brow wrinkling adorably. "I think so," she said. Her eyes widened significantly. "Oh, I see," she said. "You think destroying the back of the dress wasn't just to avoid detection? That whoever did it knew the lace on the front had special significance?"

"More than likely," Seth said. But anyone who'd spare heirloom lace certainly wasn't going to kill anyone. So why make that threat? The first two letters had expressed a desire to stop the wedding. The last had escalated to a full-on threat.

The hair on the back of his neck prickled and his palms tingled. That was the piece he'd been missing, Seth suddenly realized. Now he suspected that the last letter was written by someone else…someone who was in on the original plan but had a different agenda altogether.

The question, of course, was…who?

9

WITH THE REHEARSAL a mere eight hours away, the bride still in town searching for a new dress that didn't need much alteration, the culprits still at large, and Seth and his crew sweeping the house, Pen took a moment to do something she'd never done when she was officially at work.

She had a stiff shot of liquor.

Paul came around the corner, saw her with the bottle—who had time for a glass?—and skidded to a stop. "Whoa," he said, his eyes rounded. "It's not like you to hit the hard stuff," he said, giving his head a shake. "What's happened, Pen?"

Because they seriously didn't have a prayer in hell of keeping the destroyed dress a secret, Pen told him. She didn't, however, confide the original threat. Nor was she quite ready to confess that Seth wasn't really her boyfriend. Rather than explore the reasons behind that little nugget of unwanted insight, Pen merely ignored it.

"Her dress was destroyed? On purpose?" Paul repeated, evidently as shocked as she had been. "But why?" he asked, a perplexed scowl sliding over his face. "Why would anyone want to do that?"

"My guess is someone is trying to sabotage the wedding, keep it from happening," Pen said. Actually that wasn't a guess since she knew it for a fact, but she still didn't think she needed to tell Paul that.

Paul took the bottle from her hand and took a giant swig, wincing when it burned. "I don't blame you for drinking," he said. "So what are you going to do?"

"Carry on as usual. Trent's security team is on it," she said, hoping he wouldn't ask where Seth was. "In the interim, Nella is scouring the local area boutiques for another gown and we're going to move forward."

Paul's gaze turned speculative. "Bet you'd like to smack someone upside the head right now, wouldn't you?"

She grinned. "Are you volunteering?"

"Nope," he said, rocking back on his heels. He looked at the various tents, the white lights, the runners and pedestals that would hold the flowers when they arrived tomorrow. "It's a shame," he said. "I think this is one of the nicest shows you've ever put on."

She actually agreed. In keeping with the island theme they'd used a lot of shell colors and pale turquoise. Large fountains were erected on either side of the massive arbor, which had been built specifically for the nuptials. When the wedding was over, Trent had said he planned to put a porch swing there so that they could sit together and look out over the ocean. The property really was remarkable, Pen thought, loving the salty scent of the breeze and the live oaks, Spanish moss and oleander that littered the landscape. It was lovely and relaxing, a homey kind of paradise.

"So where's the boyfriend?" Paul finally asked. "Out fishing?"

The only person fishing around here was Paul. She felt her lips twitch. "I couldn't tell you," Pen said. "He pretty much does his own thing and let's me do mine. It's wonderful, really."

"Forward thinking, is he?" Paul remarked, clearly not buying it.

Pen suppressed a chuckle. Actually, if they'd been in a real relationship, she imagined that Seth would be a little bit old-fashioned. Despite the fact that he seemed every bit as protective of his single status as she, he nevertheless struck her as a bit traditional, for lack of a better description. He'd pulled out her chair at dinner, stood when she did and held open doors. She'd heard him use a "yes ma'am" with Trent's mother and it was as natural to him as breathing. His mother had done well with him, Pen thought. He was just reckless and irreverent enough to be utterly charming—irresistible, really—but the core values were equally evident, making him a man who was damned hard to resist.

And after that kiss last night, Pen would be the biggest kind of liar if she said she wanted to resist.

She didn't.

In fact, though she would have to worry about her equally weak flesh and moral fiber at some point in the near future, she very much wished she hadn't resisted last night. And that was a first for her. She'd met guys who'd lit her up before and, if the fire was still burning when she figured out whether or not they were worthy of sharing her body, then she typically indulged. She might be a champion dater, but she'd always been quite selective when it came to picking bed partners. It required a certain level of trust that sometimes simply never materialized.

With Seth, it had been there from the beginning. That, combined with all the other particularly compelling things about him, had made her more than a little nervous. She'd never hopped right into bed with anyone, had never had one of those all-consuming I-have-to-have-you-right-now-or-I'll-die kinds of experiences. The fact that she'd felt that kind of attraction to Seth had sent a dart of panic directly into her lust-ridden breast.

Furthermore, there wouldn't have been a bed required. She'd have been happy with a quick tumble against the wall.

Last night, rather than act on her irrational impulses, she'd played it safe and hidden in her room. And she'd been sorry all day. Why had she done that? Why had she held back when chances were that nothing like this would ever happen to her again? What were the odds that she'd ever *want* someone as much as she did right now? She knew it was her self-preservation kicking in, knew that the power that made him so appealing made him equally dangerous.

Clearly her subconscious was trying to tell her something and even more clearly, a part of her trusted him more than she trusted herself. This, she instinctively knew, was a once-in-a-lifetime opportunity and she had every intention of taking advantage of it.

After tomorrow night, whether they'd discovered who was trying to sabotage Trent and Nella's wedding or not, she'd likely never see Seth McCutcheon again. A pinprick of pain nicked her heart, making her inwardly wince with regret. She stilled as that unhappy thought wrapped itself around her chest and squeezed. A strange kind of panic sent her pulse to racing and she took the bottle of whiskey back from Paul and determinedly took another sip.

It was ridiculous, she thought, shaking off the bizarre sensation. She barely knew him. It was insane to get this worked up over someone who was as permanent as a henna tattoo.

She only regretted that she wouldn't have the time to get to know him better, Pen told herself. That was what was making her anxious. There were still so many things she didn't know about him, so many things she longed to learn. And really, considering that she'd given him so much information about herself, it hardly seemed fair that she wouldn't get at least a few answers to her questions. It was an inequitable exchange of information and the injustice irritated her, dammit. Fair was fair.

Yes, probably what she most wanted to know was none of her business, but that didn't make her any less curious. And what she wanted to know more than anything was who he'd kept his promise to. Why had their wishes been so important? Important enough for him to give up a career she instinctively knew he'd loved.

He was a walking puzzle and she longed to make the pieces fit.

Preferably his pieces into hers.

"That was a quick recovery," Paul remarked, staring at her with an uncomfortable amount of shrewdness. "A minute ago you looked like someone had kicked your dog. Now you're smiling." He nodded to the bottle and quirked a brow. "That must be magic liquor."

"I don't know about that, but it's good."

Paul frowned. "Where'd you get it?"

"From my secret stash."

"Which is?"

"Secret," Pen told him. "Now get to work. We've got a wedding to pull off."

Grumbling good-naturedly about whip-wielding bosses, Paul went over and started helping the caterer move the tables into place. She'd provided a diagram, of course, but her attention to detail was one of the main things that had contributed to her success. Typically people did what they said they were going to do, but invariably mistakes were made. It was her job to fix them before they became major problems.

The fact that she wasn't doing anything to help Trent and Nella find out who was behind the threats had weighed on her more than she'd like to admit. Feeling useless wasn't a problem she was used to having. Her gaze stole to the house, where Seth and the other Ranger Security guys were busy doing their part and an idea suddenly struck.

The cars.

She could do a little recon of her own. Under the

guise of letting Pen know whether or not Nella had found a replacement dress, Nella was supposed to give her an estimated time of arrival. With any luck, Nella and her bridesmaids would be gone long enough for Seth and his men to do a thorough search of the house and the vehicles.

She was going to help them out with those.

Though she knew no one was watching her, she nevertheless peeked around and then quickly made her way to the driveway. Thankfully, Lucy had driven, her mother with her, and she could take a quick peek inside to see if anything looked suspicious. Crouching low, she carefully opened the door of the sporty sedan and slid into the passenger seat. She looked around, noting the overall tidiness of the interior—no straw wrappers or stray French fries here, she thought—and decided to start with the glove compartment. Insurance papers, tag receipts, air freshener and a few pens. Nothing damning whatsoever.

She moved to the console and found a lot of CDs— Lucy was a Lady Gaga fan, evidently—and a small sewing kit, first-aid kit and mini-digital recorder. The latter was intriguing but, while she was intensely curious about what might be on the device, she simply couldn't justify playing it. She was looking for a red permanent marker and a sharp instrument. Deliberately listening to the recording without just cause felt more like spying and less like being helpful. She spent a few more minutes checking the side pockets and underneath the seats, but didn't find anything.

Dejected, she quietly slipped out of the car and headed over to Patrice's SUV.

AFTER AN ULTIMATELY futile search, Seth met Will, Tanner and Huck in the foyer of Trent's house. All four of them were frustrated and, like Seth, knew that time was running out. If they didn't figure out who was behind this at some point before the wedding, then in all likelihood, there *wouldn't* be a wedding.

Because he'd lost all perspective, he was actually more concerned about the consequences to Pen's business than Trent and Nella's marital plans. If push came to shove, Trent and Nella could always go to the courthouse and get married. But Pen's career would go into a tailspin. Everything she'd worked for, all the successful events she'd competently hosted would be largely forgotten in the wake of a high-profile mishap.

That was simply unacceptable.

Even though he knew that he was technically working for Trent, Seth found himself more aligned with protecting Pen's interests than those of his employer. It was a good damned thing that they weren't mutually exclusive, he thought, trying to ignore the significance of that particular revelation.

"You know what the problem is, don't you?" Huck asked them. "It's women. Women are diabolical," he told them, his face twisting with equal parts admiration and disgust. "Which, admittedly can be attractive in a weird sort of way, but in this instance, it's proving to be damned inconvenient."

"Damned straight," Tanner agreed. "I can't believe

we've put the man-hours into this that we have, only to narrow it down to a couple of amateur females who are, quite honestly, getting the better of us." He grinned. "Not that I could share that opinion in front of my wife, mind you. She'd accuse me of being sexist. Which I'm not…really," he qualified with a sheepish smile.

"Sexist or not, we're former military," Will chimed in. "Official badasses and look at us," he said, gesturing to the lot of them. "Bested by a chick with a red pen and a razor. It's despicable."

Tanner chuckled. "Given the choice between tangling with a woman or an insurgent, I'd take the insurgent any day."

A low laugh rumbled up Seth's throat. "I think that's a choice we'd all make," he said. "But unfortunately that's not the option we're presented with." He looked at Will. "Will, I want you to run a check on the cell phones and see if you find anything that looks suspicious."

Will nodded. "On it."

He looked at Tanner and Huck. "Both women have laptops and we're rapidly running out of time. Can you—"

"Of course," Huck said, nodding decisively.

Tanner quirked a brow. "What about the mother's?"

Seth did another gut check. "I think she's clear, but better safe than sorry. Do Patrice's first," he said, thinking that hers was the most likely hit. "I'm going to go out and check the cars. Let me know if you find anything, anything at all, regardless how insignificant it might seem. If it gives you pause, I want to know. Let's meet back down at the pier in an hour. We'll pretend to be admiring the boat."

"I won't have to pretend," he heard Will say as he walked away. "That baby is beautiful."

Smiling, Seth made his way outside and around to the parking area. The sedan belonged to Lucy and the SUV to Patrice. Thinking that the SUV would take longer, Seth decided to work that one first. He opened the door and a woman screamed, frightening him more thoroughly than he'd ever admit. Damned rookie mistake. He should have looked first. But he'd had no reason to. Or so he'd thought. He swore and climbed quickly into the backseat of the vehicle where the windows were better tinted.

"What the hell are you doing?" he whispered furiously at Pen.

"You scared the hell out of me!" She had a hand pressed to her heart and she was struggling to get her breathing under control. Once she did, she looked at him and evidently found something incredibly funny. Because she started laughing and couldn't stop. "You should have seen the l-look on your f-face," she wheezed. "I think I scared you as much as you scared me."

He'd risk dismemberment before he'd admit it, but chuckled despite himself. Then he glared at her and tried to look formidable. "I think you're mistaken."

"And I think you're full of shit."

He felt his eyes widen and a laugh rumbled up his throat. "I can see no way of responding to that without being crude, so I won't." He stared at her, trying hard to ignore the way her breasts strained against the filmy sundress she currently wore and the way her hair was spilling over her creamy shoulders. Whatever perfume she was wearing was doubly intoxicating in the warm car—thank God it had been parked in the shade—and he could feel it curling around his senses, playing hell with his brain.

"What are you doing out here?" he asked, struggling to focus.

She swallowed, the fine muscles in her throat moving deliciously. He was suddenly hit with the urge to lick the hollow in her neck, slide his tongue along the sleek indentations of her collarbone. It was finely made, like delicate wings spanning shoulder to shoulder.

"I had a few minutes and wanted to help," she said. "You'd mentioned searching the cars, so…"

He was torn between being impressed with her dedication to her couple and furious over the fact that she'd interfered. You didn't see him trying to help her plan the wedding, did you? He almost pointed that out, but admiration won out and he merely sighed. "Look, Pen, I appreciate it, but you really need to leave this to me and my team."

She hesitated. "We're running out of time," she said. "If we don't get to the bottom of this tonight, then I'm afraid that something truly horrible is going to happen. That someone will call the pastor and tell him the wedding is off again, that someone will ruin the cake, or cut up Trent's tux or spray weed killer all over the flowers. There are so many things that could go wrong between now and I-do time and I—" She looked away and her hands fisted tightly in her lap. "I'm not trying to step on your toes, Seth," she said, shooting him a look. "I know I'm a control freak. I know that I tend to go a wee bit overboard on things—"

He snorted before he could help himself and she punched him playfully in the arm.

"But I just can't sit around and do nothing. Not when I see an opportunity to be useful."

He stilled and continued to stare at her, then his throat grew tight. He knew someone else who always had a need to be useful, Seth thought. And his mother would have loved Penelope. She would have admired her wit, her work ethic and her sense of humor.

She studied him and her smile slowly capsized. "Did I say something wrong?"

"No," he said, looking away. "And I do understand that you want to help, but…"

She grinned. "But you don't need my help."

"I didn't say that." And he wouldn't, because it would be unkind and, really, not altogether true. At this point he should be willing to take all the help he could get. "So have you found anything?" he asked.

"Not yet," she admitted. "I went through Lucy's car first and, other than a digital voice recorder in the console, I didn't find anything interesting at all."

"A digital voice recorder?" he said. "Lucy isn't a doctor, right? She's a massage therapist, isn't she?" Why would she need a voice recorder? Seth wondered.

"Right."

"Did you listen to it?"

"No," she said, wincing regretfully. "I just couldn't

bring myself to do it. It seems like such an invasion of privacy."

That wasn't a problem for him, Seth thought. Given what had been going on and that his gut was telling him Trent's sister was somehow involved, he didn't have a problem crossing that line. In fact, given the stakes, as far as he was concerned there was no line.

"What about in here?" he asked.

"Nothing so far," she said, moistening her lips. Her gaze dropped to his mouth, then found his eyes again. "We should probably start looking."

If they didn't, he was going to start something else. And, though there was a condom in his wallet, there was precious little room back here. Still…

He nodded, trying to focus on something besides the sweet plumpness of her breasts swelling beneath the fabric of her dress, the teeny bit of cleavage visible when she moved just so. His mouth watered.

They shared a long look, then both of them bolted into action, leaning toward the front of the car at the same time.

Her "ow" was met with his "damn" and they fell back and looked at each other, then started laughing again. He loved that she laughed so easily, so open and honest and unrestrained. She rubbed her temple and he moved her hand so that he could take a look. "Sorry about that," he said, still chuckling.

She was fine—no blood and no bump—but this close he could smell her shampoo and he was loath to move away from her.

"You have a hard head," she said, laughing softly.

That wasn't the only thing that was hard at the moment. "So I've been told," he murmured, drawing back to better look at her. He paused and gave her a significant look. He was quickly losing what little grip he'd managed to keep on his self-control. "One of us is going to have to get out of the car," he said. "Otherwise I'm going to start something and I'm not going to want to stop."

She swallowed. "Is that a warning?"

"It's a fact," he said, laying it all out on the line for her. He wanted her more than he'd ever wanted another woman in his life. He wanted to eat her up and breathe her in and taste every single inch of her. He wanted to fill his mouth with her breasts and feel her small hands sliding over his bare back. He wanted to slip that dress out of the way and pull her into his lap and settle her down on top of him. He wanted to take her hard and fast and slake a bit of his lust and then take her again and savor her slowly.

Every muscle in his body was aching with pent-up need and he was rapidly losing the ability to keep himself away from her, to keep from merely touching his lips to hers—a single touch was all he needed—and then doing exactly what he wanted to do with her.

And the kicker? The cherry on top? What lit him up more than anything else?

She wanted it, too. He could her feel the tension, her need rebounding off his own. It was a damned miracle the heat between them hadn't set the car ablaze.

She looked up at him from beneath a sweep of sooty lashes, her blue eyes dark with desire and the thrill of a challenge. She quirked a sleek brow and her voice, when she spoke, was throaty and low. "What makes you think I'm going to ask you to stop?"

10

IT WAS THE RAW NEED in the warning that ultimately did it for her, Pen thought. His bold green gaze raked over her as though she was a feast for the senses—*his*, in particular—and he was a starving man.

Which was fine with her, because she was starving too. Her body was too sensitive, too tight and too damned hot. The pure desire pumping through her veins was unlike anything she'd ever experienced before. She couldn't believe they were about to do it in a car, particularly one that didn't belong to either of them, but ultimately, she didn't care. Nothing mattered, least of all propriety. Her hands craved him, her very skin ached for his touch, and the low, steady throb hitting her womb with every beat of her heart all but had her squirming in the seat.

She wanted. *Him*.

He chuckled low and his gaze drifted over her face, then settled on her mouth. "Well, in that case," he murmured silkily, his voice rough like velvet against satin as he pushed his big hand into her hair, cupped the back of her neck and brought her mouth to his.

She simultaneously sighed and burned, and a long tremor of anticipation resonated down her spine.

This, she knew, was going to be beyond good.

He kissed her, softly at first, just a mere brush of his lips against hers. His other hand found her face, cupping her jaw. The strength and desire and something else not altogether readable, but profound nonetheless, made her insides quiver and melt.

His tongue tangled around hers, stroking the soft recesses of her mouth, his lips molding perfectly to her own, creating the perfect amount of moisture between them. An elusive trick that, Pen thought dimly as her aching breasts brushed against his magnificent chest. A dry kiss was awkward and too much spit made her gag, but he… She pulled him closer to her, desperate to be nearer. He knew what he was doing.

Pen cradled his face between her hands and savored the feel of his jaw against her palms. Seeing good bone structure and masculine skin was no substitute for actually touching it. Feeling the curve of a jaw, the delicious prick of stubble beneath her hand…wonderful.

He gently tugged her closer, shifting her until she straddled him and the first bit of pressure against her sex had her squirming shamelessly against him. Breathing raggedly, he tore his mouth away from hers and licked a path down her throat, causing a wave of gooseflesh to skitter over her arms. His mouth followed the line along her shoulder and she gasped and held him closer, pushing her hands into his hair, along the strangely soft skin behind his ears.

She felt his big hands slide down her back, along the edge of her spine. They settled possessively on her rump and gave a gentle squeeze. She shifted against him, aligning herself more firmly against the thick ridge straining against his shorts. Her sex wept, readying for him, and he pushed up, nudging her swollen clit. She gasped and he used the distraction to his advantage, slipping her breast from the built-in cup of her sundress.

"No bra," he murmured against her nipple before laving it and pulling it into his hot mouth.

"No need," Pen managed, the breath thinning in her lungs as pleasure arced through her. "It's part of the dress."

He freed her other breast. "Ingenious," he said, then pulled the bud into his mouth, flattening the sensitive crown against the roof of his mouth. His hands slipped her dress out of the way, putting skin against skin, and the first touch of those greedy palms against her bare rear made a shudder rip through her.

He drew back, his eyes heavy lidded and sexy, and he grinned, seemingly impressed. "No panties, either?"

"Thong," she said, chuckling.

"An itty-bitty thong," he remarked, his hands sliding higher until he found the minuscule straps. "Ah," he sighed knowingly. "This is almost indecent," he murmured. His green eyes twinkled with admiration. "I like that in a woman."

"You know what I like in a pretend boyfriend?"

"I hate to disappoint you, baby, but I don't wear thongs," he said, kissing her again.

She chuckled against his mouth and shifted so that she could find the snap of his shorts. His zipper whined and, with the smallest amount of maneuvering, he sprang free right into her waiting hand.

She'd been right. He was *definitely* well proportioned.

He was hot and hard and thick. Her mouth watered and her feminine muscles clenched in anticipation of feeling him there, deep within her, pushing and pulsing and taking her to the top of Orgasm Mountain and then shoving her off, so that she could free-fall through the sensation. That's what she wanted, what she needed. She—

Her cell phone suddenly sounded, the tune of "Going to the Chapel" echoing like a gunshot in the hot SUV.

Seth swore. "What the fu—"

Pen scrambled for her phone and checked the display. "It's a text from Nella," she said. "She found a dress and they'll be here in about thirty minutes. They ended up in Foley."

Seth leaned forward and kissed her again, pushing up against her once more, snatching the breath from her lungs. Her eyes practically rolled back in her head. "Then I guess we'd better hurry," he said. "But give me five seconds." He called Will and gave him Nella's ETA. Once that little bit of business was concluded, he found his wallet and drew a condom out. He tore the package open with his teeth, then quickly withdrew the protection. She took it from him and rolled it into place.

It was a tight fit.

Sweet mercy… He was magnificent.

"I like it when your eyes go all sleepy," he told her as she leaned forward and felt him nudge her entrance. He swept her panties aside, moving them out of the way. Every vital organ in her body shook from that small contact and she dimly wondered what would happen when he was inside her. If she'd simply fly apart on the inside, her skin the only thing holding her together.

He framed her face with his hands and bent forward and kissed her again. Then he moved his hands down, lingering over her rear and sliding up her back, his thumbs skimming her spine. Though, at five-two, Pen was used to feeling small, he made her feel positively dainty and breakable. The need and reverence in his touch was something she'd never felt before, a lethal combo that could truly screw up her heart if she wasn't careful.

But it was a little late for being careful, Pen thought, sliding slowly down onto him. Her eyes fluttered shut and her breath, when it finally returned, leaked weakly out of her lungs. He was… She could…

Oh, my.

She looked at Seth and his teeth were bared in a primal sort of smile, one that sent a thrill through her. She tightened around him, then lifted up once more and moaned on the way back down.

He made a low masculine growl in the back of his throat and then bent forward and licked a path between her breasts. Then he moved over and wrapped his lips around her nipple, laving it with his tongue.

She inexplicably tightened around him, and repeated the process over again. Up and then down, slowly undulating her hips so that she took all of him inside her, feeling every long, hot inch of him deep in her core.

He was like a drug winding through her blood, Pen thought, her entire body simultaneously energized and languid, the poison and the antidote. And as much as she'd like to draw this out, to milk every bit of sensation slowly and thoroughly from their bodies, she could feel the quickening in her sex, the tingling herald of impending orgasm. She upped her tempo, riding him harder, her hands anchored on his shoulders. She should have taken his shirt off, Pen thought, absently and made a mental note for next time. She wanted to taste that bare skin, feel it beneath her tongue.

Recognizing her intent—what she needed—Seth arched up beneath her. He caught her rhythm and pounded into her, his hands on either side of her hips, holding her while he made her his. With each flex of his hips, she felt him claiming her, branding her, marking his territory…ruining her for anyone else.

That terrifying thought echoed through her head at the exact moment the orgasm finally crested and she free-fell through the exquisite sensation. Her breath caught in her throat, her mouth opened in a soundless scream, and every muscle in her body tightened as the pleasure exploded inside her.

She happened to look down at him, saw the satisfied gleam in his eye, the masculine pleasure, and the crooked grin on his beautiful lips and knew she was in terrible, terrible trouble.

Because though she was resistant to the idea, she had the horrible suspicion that she was falling for her pretend boyfriend.

Thankfully, he wasn't finished yet, so the worry fled as quickly as it had come. And then he kissed her again and she stopped thinking altogether.

BLACK CURLS spilling around her creamy shoulders, plump breasts tipped with pouty pale pink nipples, her teeth sunk into that full bottom lip as she rose and fell on top of him, his dick surrounded by her tight warmth...

He'd died and gone to heaven, Seth thought. Or he'd been transported to paradise, because she was the most responsive, most beautiful creature he'd ever had the pleasure to take to bed.

Or take in the car, actually, he thought, wishing they had a lot more room and a limitless amount of time to explore and play, to sample and taste.

Honestly, when she'd looked at him and said "What makes you think I'm going to ask you to stop?" he'd gone from being painfully hard to near immaculate ejaculation. He could feel the desperation in her touch, her desire mingling with his own and there was nothing— *nothing*—more attractive than a woman who wanted you, who wanted to get beneath your skin, who genuinely with-every-fiber-of-her-being *had to have* you.

He'd been getting that vibe from Penelope from the instant she'd appeared on his doorstep. And, though he wished they could have done this last night like he'd wanted to, he damned sure wasn't going to complain.

How could he, when she was riding him like this? When she'd just come for him and, with any luck, he was going to make her do it again. He thrust up into her, over and over again, taking her harder and faster, her sweet channel squeezing him, seemingly trying to keep him inside of her body. Her heavy breasts bounced on her chest, her nipples pearled tight, begging for his kiss.

He bent forward and drew one into his mouth, raked the hard tip against his tongue and felt her shudder. He could feel his own release building in the back of his loins, gathering force with every delicious draw and drag between their joined bodies.

"Seth," she gasped, and he loved the way his name came off her lips, all breathy and feminine and low.

"Pen," he returned, kissing the underside of her jaw. She smelled like ginger, he realized, finally isolating the scent. Ginger and musk and cloves. It was earthy and provocative and he enjoyed how it rose off her skin and slid into his lungs.

"I don't know if I can—" She moaned and clung to him, her breath hitching. "I... Please... Now—"

And there we go, Seth thought, the moment he'd been waiting for. He pushed high and angled deep, then reached between them and stroked the nub nestled at the top of her slippery sex.

She shattered around him, her feminine muscles clenching tight once more. That was all it took to send him hurtling over the edge. He let go and came hard and when he would have quit, she kept going, kept squeezing, kept rocking above him, pulling every bit of sensation from him that she could.

She was thorough, his pretend girlfriend, Seth thought, and every muscle in his body went limp.

Best. Orgasm. Ever.

Ever.

She handed him a tissue—thankfully Patrice had a box on hand—and he quickly disposed of the condom. Or disposed of it as best he could until he could find a garbage can. He couldn't very well leave it in the car, Seth thought, stifling a smile. That would be bad form. Evidently reading his thoughts, Pen grabbed another handful of tissues, wrapped up the evidence and, grimacing slightly, stowed it in her purse.

She rested her forehead against his, heaved a big sigh and smiled. "I'm glad we got that out of the way," she said, much to his surprise.

A startled laugh rumbled from his chest. "You make me sound like something on your to-do list."

Her smile turned wicked. "You were and I just did you, so…" She lifted a shoulder in a little shrug.

Feigning outrage, he wrapped a black curl around his finger and tugged. "Where is this damned list?" he asked her. "I need to make sure that I'm penciled in a few more times."

She chuckled. "Oh, I think that can be arranged."

He grinned, pleased. "After the rehearsal dinner tonight?"

She grimaced. "Provided there is a rehearsal dinner. Did you find anything in the house?" she asked.

He shook his head. "Not yet. We're still checking a

few things like the computers and cell records, but so far, we haven't come across anything that's going to be solid evidence."

A worried frown worked its way across her brow and he slid a finger over the line, smoothing it away.

She smiled and something about that grin made his chest constrict, made his heart skip a beat, and the prelude to something he didn't fully understand yawned before him. *One of these days you're going to find your rudder...and I hope she initially mops the deck with you.* Nah, Seth told himself. He was being ridiculous. He'd just met Penelope, they barely knew each other. He couldn't—

"I guess we'd better get back to work," she said, reluctantly climbing off him.

Still trying to recover from that bizarre premonition, Seth buttoned his shorts and made an effort to focus. It took more concentration than he was accustomed to, which only served to rattle him further. "Right," he said. "So where have you looked?"

"In the glove box, the side pockets and console," she said.

He smiled at her. "Are you going to be insulted if I go behind you?"

She rolled her eyes. "And people call *me* a control freak."

"You are a control freak," he said, slipping into the front seat so that he could better search.

"And you're not?"

"Nope. I'm a perfectionist. There's a difference."

She snorted. "You're so full of—"

"Hey," he interrupted, shooting her a look as he closed the glove box. As she'd said, it had yielded nothing. "I didn't say it was a bad thing. In fact, I happen to think it's one of those endearing quirks you mentioned before."

She looked momentarily startled, then she smiled. "Er…thanks. I think."

He chuckled and moved to the console. Several CDs, a few pens, a package of cigarettes that smelled curiously like vanilla, a notebook that revealed only the odd address, phone number and grocery list. Nothing that said, *I'm guilty!* unfortunately.

Pen had practically turned herself upside down to look under the backseat and he chuckled softly, admiring the view. "Anything under there?"

"Only some loose change and a flashlight," came her slightly muffled reply.

Seth checked the passenger-side door compartment and found a lone French fry and a packet of salt, then moved to the driver's side. There was an atlas, more CD cases, a receipt from Starbucks and a Jolly Rancher candy. That was it. Getting more and more frustrated and less and less confident of actually being able to catch either Patrice, Lucy or even Nella's mother, for that matter, Seth swore.

"It's looking bad, isn't it?" she said, righting herself. Her pink cheeks puffed as she exhaled heavily, her lips still swollen from his kisses.

He'd been better off not to notice that, because it just made him want to kiss her again. Sadly, though, they really didn't have the time. The clock was ticking and they were no closer to outing the villain than they'd been when Nella and the others left.

Pen's phone rang again, this time to the tune of the theme music from *Jaws.* "Monica," she explained with a wry smile in answer to his questioning gaze.

The *Jaws* theme music? he thought, smothering another laugh. Did she have a special ring tone for everyone? he wondered. If so, what would she choose for him?

"Yes, Mon?" She looked at him and grinned. "Where am I? I'm here. Where are you?" A pause then, "Er…no. Is there a problem? No? Then why are you—" Another pause. "I'm not AWOL, dammit. I'm helping Seth." He could hear Monica's laugh over the phone and he had the pleasure of watching Pen blush to the roots of her hair. "Monica, we're quite busy right now, so—" She moaned and snapped the phone shut. "Nosy help," she muttered. "*I'm* the boss here," she ranted quietly. "A fact she frequently forgets."

"She seems to have a great deal of admiration for you," Seth said. Her entire staff did, in fact, as well as anyone else he'd met who'd worked with her in any capacity.

"But a little too much familiarity for my liking," she said, shooting him a smile.

Seth climbed back over to where she was sitting, then leaned over that seat as well and inspected the cargo area. To his delight, he could feel her gaze on his ass.

"You can touch it if you want," he told her.

"Sorry?"

Rather than tease her, he lifted the small hold in

the bottom of the cargo area and shook his head when there was nothing there. He'd still sweep Lucy's car but felt certain he wasn't going to find anything of significance.

He hauled himself back over and settled heavily into the seat, then muttered a low curse under his breath. Okay, Seth told himself. Time to move on to something else, to check in and see if the others had found anything at all. He leaned over and kissed Pen again and it took more strength than he'd guessed to pull away. His will was getting weaker and weaker where she was concerned.

Gratifyingly, her eyes were dark with longing when he drew back.

"We'd better get moving," he said.

She nodded, then leaned forward to put the tissue box back where they'd found it. An odd look passed over her face when she picked it up and, rather than set it down, she brought it closer and gave it a shake.

Something rattled from inside the box and they shared a look.

She reached in and withdrew a slim X-Acto knife, the kind with the retractable blade. White fibers had been caught between the casing and the knife when the blade had been pulled into the safety position.

She inhaled sharply. "Patrice," she breathed, clearly stunned.

The smoking gun that wasn't, Seth thought.

But it was all the evidence they needed.

To nail her, anyway.

11

STILL REELING from the fact that Patrice was obviously behind everything, Pen scrambled out of the car, both hot and heartsick. How could Patrice do this? What on earth would possess her to try to ruin her friend's wedding? She'd hosted Nella's shower, for heaven's sake! She'd helped pick out the bridesmaids' dresses and put together the menu. What would make her *destroy* Nella's dress? The letters she could almost see. If she was simply trying to stop the wedding, then the threats were an annoyance, but not destructive or malicious.

Ripping the back of that dress to ribbons was both.

She could personally throttle Patrice with *both* hands as well.

Seth immediately got on his cell phone. "I've got an X-Acto knife with white fibers attached," he said. "We found it in Patrice's car."

She liked that he'd included her in that, Pen thought, wishing that she had more time to linger over the fact that they'd had the most amazing sex of her life. Unfortunately, when this weekend was over, she'd have plenty of time. But for the moment, Trent and Nella's wedding had to come first.

"You did," she heard him say. "Well, that's an interesting development," he said, shooting her an enigmatic look. Good grief, he was unbelievably good-looking. She knew it was an inopportune moment to be thinking that, but she couldn't seem to help herself.

What? she mouthed, hating being left out of the loop, even for an instant.

"Right. In the laptop case. Anything on the computer?" A pause then. "No shit," he breathed, looking utterly blindsided. "Wow. I, uh…I certainly hadn't seen that coming, had you?"

"What?" Pen asked more loudly. The suspense was killing her. They rounded the corner and came face-to-face with the other security agents, all of them looking slightly bemused.

Seth and Will snapped their phones shut. "We've got about ten minutes before they arrive," Will said, and looked to Seth. "How are we going to handle this?"

"First order of business is to tell Trent," Seth said. "We need to brief him completely and then see what he thinks about Lucy's involvement."

Pen gasped. "Lucy?"

"Will found a red marker in her laptop bag and a few of the wedding invitations and save-the-date announcements she'd practiced on first."

Oh, no, Pen thought. Poor Trent! Poor Nella! One of her best friends and her future sister-in-law. "Were they acting independently, or were they in it together?" Pen asked.

"One of them was acting independently," Seth said. "The other one was being coerced." She watched him glance significantly to the other men. "And there's still one unaccounted for."

She was developing a terrible headache and felt slightly sick to her stomach. "Please tell me Lucy was the one being coerced." Friends were hard to lose, but marrying into a family where the association would be constant, the betrayal always fresh…that would be utterly terrible. And one unaccounted for? What was he talking about? They'd found the pen and invitations in Lucy's bag and the knife in Patrice's car. That was everything, wasn't it?

"Lucy was being coerced," Seth confirmed. "But the circumstances are…not good," he finished. That sounded exceedingly ominous, Pen thought. "What do you mean one is still unaccounted for?"

"I don't think Lucy wrote the third note," he said, looking at Tanner. "Think about it. The first two were simply instructions to call it off, expressing displeasure. The last one was written in the same style—so this person knew it was happening—but it had a completely different tone. I think we're dealing with someone else here."

Tanner winced and the rest of the them shared a look. "Good spot," he told Seth. "I think you're right."

"Anyone who would spare the lace on the front of the dress isn't going to kill someone," Seth continued. "So that rules out Patrice. Did you find anything at all on the computers?"

"Other than what we told you on the phone, no," Huck told him.

Pen's head was spinning. Everything Seth had said made perfect sense. Something else was going on, something worse than what Lucy and Patrice had done. But who was responsible? And what was their motive?

Having been for a walk down along the beach, Trent and his mother strolled into view and both of them looked up when they saw everyone gathered in front of the house. Trent put a hand to his mother's elbow and they hurried forward.

"Trent, I need a word," Seth told him.

Trent's mother lifted her chin. "I will not be left in the dark anymore," she said. "My son has filled me in, quite reluctantly," she added, shooting him a pointed glare which displayed her displeasure. "But that is done. Whatever you say to him, you can say in front of me, right, Trent?"

Penelope could tell that Seth did not want to share his news in front of Trent's mother. Especially if it involved Lucy.

Trent finally nodded, though a muscle worked in his jaw. "Go ahead," he said. "I've told her everything else."

And he'd caught hell for keeping it from her, if Pen had to guess.

Seth held up the knife with the white threads caught in the case and Trent's eyes widened. "We found this hidden in a box of tissues in Patrice's SUV," he said.

"Patrice?" his mother breathed, obviously stunned. "Patrice did that?"

Will held up the red marker and winced. "And we found this in your sister's laptop case, along with these," he added, showing the trial efforts Lucy had made on their wedding announcements.

Trent's mother blanched and for a moment, she looked as if she was going to faint. Pen hurried forward and slid an arm around the women's waist. "Are you all right, Mrs. McWilliams?"

"Lucy," she said faintly. Her brow furrowed and for the first time, she looked older than her years. "Lucy is involved in this?" She looked at Trent. "But she loves Nella. She's been looking forward to finally having a sister. Why?" she asked. "It makes no sense. Are you certain? Could they have been planted there?"

Seth winced and shook his head. "She was coerced."

Trent's shrewd gaze narrowed. "Coerced? You mean blackmailed?"

Seth nodded again, looking even grimmer than he had before, if that was possible, and Pen knew the "not good" he'd alluded to earlier was going to be revealed soon. Much as she wanted to know, there was a part of her that was dreading it as well. She tightened her grip on Mrs. McWilliams.

"By Patrice?" Trent asked.

"Yes," Seth told him. "Patrice's former husband was a—" he struggled for moment "—*client* of your sister, and Patrice found out."

Both Pen and Mrs. McWilliams caught on before Trent did and Mrs. McWilliams sagged against her. "Oh, dear God. You don't mean…please don't tell me…"

Lucy was a call girl? Quiet, unassuming Lucy? Timid Lucy who always kowtowed to her mother was a *call girl?*

Trent's eyes suddenly widened with comprehension and then his jaw went slack. "What do you mean when you say *client?*"

Seth coughed uncomfortably. "I mean she was giving more than the traditional massage to certain customers."

Trent looked stunned.

His mother's mind was a lot quicker.

"Are you obligated to report this to the authorities?" she asked, looking directly at Seth.

"No," Seth told her. He didn't look to the others, and for whatever reason, she got the distinct impression that he'd made that call on his own.

"I still don't understand why Patrice would have objected to the wedding?" Trent said, still obviously struggling with the fact that his little sister had become a hooker. "Why should she care whether or not Nella and I get married?"

"According to the emails I found on Lucy's computer, Patrice was merely trying to save Nella future heartache," Will told him. "She doesn't believe any man is capable of being faithful. She enlisted your sister's help as payback and has been threatening to out her if she didn't cooperate. Lucy chose the lesser of two evils and aligned herself with Patrice."

By the look on Trent's mother's face, that was going to be a move Lucy would live to regret.

Seth looked at Trent. "They'll be here in a minute. How do you want to handle this?"

"Does Patrice have actual proof of Lucy's…indiscretions?"

Will shook his head. "I don't think so. I think her ex-husband admitted it, but I don't think she has anything concrete."

And Patrice's ex certainly wasn't going to give her proof, Pen thought.

Trent nodded. "Then I want Patrice escorted off the island with express instructions never to contact myself or my wife again," he said. "If she does, there will be consequences."

"Trent, Nella—"

"I'll talk to Nella, Mom," he said.

"But what if Nella wants to confront her?"

Trent merely smiled and shook his head. "Believe me, when I tell her what Patrice has done, Nella's not going to ever want to talk to her again." He glanced at Pen. "You know Nella, Penelope. What do you think?"

"I think you've got her figured out pretty good," Pen said. And he was right. Nella would absolutely wash her hands of Patrice after this. She wouldn't waste her time listening to any excuses. There was nothing that could be said that would exonerate the behavior.

"And Lucy?" Seth asked.

"I'll take care of her," Mrs. McWilliams said, her voice filled with significantly ominous undertones.

Seth nodded. "All right. We'll look after Patrice, then," he assured Trent.

Trent looked up and cast his gaze around the group.

"Listen, thanks guys. I know this has been a pain in the ass, but I really appreciate the work you've done here."

"You're more than welcome," Seth told him. "But we're not done," he said. He recounted his suspicion that the third note was done by someone else. "We've still got to nail that person—which we will—then see you safely married, without interruption from any crazed fans."

"I'm nervous about those twins," Tanner piped up. It was common knowledge that a pair of identical twins from Miami somehow managed to streak naked across the field during a playoff game. Of course, if you asked Pen, security had been purposely lax on that because the girls were quite pretty.

Trent's mother gave a disgusted grunt. "Harlots," she said, her nose wrinkling in distaste. "If they even think about streaking through this wedding, I'll personally take a birch to them."

Seth's lips twitched and the other three managed to turn their laughs into semiconvincing coughs. "We'll see to it that nothing happens, Mrs. McWilliams."

She nodded, seemingly satisfied.

"All right, then," Seth said. "I think we should be waiting with Patrice's things and vehicle at the security gate." He glanced at Huck. "Can you get clean out her room?"

Huck nodded and hurried inside. After a moment, the other two followed him. "I'll meet you at her car in two," Seth hollered over his shoulder.

"Are you going to tell Nella about Lucy's part in this?" Trent's mother asked her son.

"Of course," he said. "She's my going to be my wife. I can't keep this from her."

"But—"

"Nella comes first, Mom. Lucy should have thought about that before she allowed herself to be maneuvered into this."

"But this will hurt Nella, too," his mother argued.

"It will," he admitted. "And that makes me even angrier at Lucy."

With that comment, he turned and walked into the house.

Penelope had met many couples and had been blown away before by their devotion, but she'd never seen anything as honorable as what she'd just witnessed. He was standing by his bride, his soon-to-be wife, and nothing was going to prevent him from doing what was right by her, even if it meant hurting her in the process.

That took guts. And a helluva lot of love.

For the first time, Mrs. McWilliams seemed to truly accept the change coming into their lives. Trent's father had died when Trent was in his teens and since then, Trent had been the head of the family. And he'd just let his mother know that he would still be the head of the family. Only Nella would be his second in command, not his mother or his sister.

Evidently needing a moment to herself, Mrs. McWilliams turned and made her way back toward the beach.

Seth turned to Penelope, his expression one that was

hard to read. Relief, but with a little regret, no doubt on Trent's behalf, thrown in for good measure. "Well," he said. "This has been quite a day."

She smiled and crossed her arms over her chest. "It certainly has." She paused. "You know what this means, don't you?"

He arched a brow. "Am I supposed to?"

"It means that I'm down at least one, potentially *two*, bridesmaids."

Seth chuckled and slid a finger down the side of her cheek. "I have every confidence that you'll take care of that."

"Should I wait for Nella?"

Seth shook his head. "Let Trent handle it. Once she's absorbed everything, she'll come to you."

The other three Rangers came back outside and they headed off to Patrice's car. As if on cue, Pen's cell phone played the *Jaws* music again.

What a friggin' day. And it wasn't even half over yet.

Despite the fact that they'd successfully solved part of the problem, Seth couldn't shake the sensation that the other shoe was about to drop, that something terrible was in the works. He scanned the crowd gathered for the rehearsal, searching for anything that looked suspect or out of place. All of these people were supposed to be here. Nevertheless, one of them was still a threat.

Though he didn't want to trod on his new coworkers' toes, a part of him wanted to scan the house again, to look with his own eyes. He particularly wanted to look at Patrice's cell records and to do another scan of Lucy's laptop. Something was bothering him, but he couldn't put his finger on what.

He strolled over to Tanner. "Can you watch things for a minute," he said. "I want to go check something out."

Tanner nodded. "Sure. We'll cover."

Making sure that Lucy, who looked completely miserable, was safely out of the way, Seth made his way back to her car and pulled the digital recorder out of the console. He hit Play and recognized Patrice's voice at once. "You'll do as I say, Lucy, you miserable home-wrecking whore, or I'll make you pay." She chuckled softly. "Or rather *he* will."

He? Who was he?

"Patrice, I've already told you I was sorry. I don't know what else to do. I don't know how to make this right."

"You can't make it right. You've ruined my life. But *he* understands and he's willing to love me, even though he knows I can't love him as much in return. And he blames you, Lucy. He blames *you*." Another eerie laugh. "I'd watch my back if I were you."

He? Seth wondered again. Who in the hell had she been talking about? Furthermore, why hadn't Lucy mentioned this to any of them? When confronted, she'd only said that Patrice had been threatening her and they just assumed that, based on the emails, that it was only in regard to the call girl service. But obviously, it had been more.

Significantly more, based on what he'd just heard.

A terrible sense of unease washing over him, Seth rounded the corner and almost walked into Paul, who was leaning against the house smoking another cigarette.

The scent of vanilla hit him, triggering a memory from Patrice's car. Suddenly, Seth knew he had him.

So did Paul and, with a muttered curse, he took off.

Shouting a loud "Get him!", Seth ran after him. The Ranger Security men were the only ones who didn't react with complete confusion. They took off after Paul as well. But like them, their suspect was fit and former military and he was damned light on his feet. He hurried through the crowd like a seasoned running back and then grabbed Lucy, whirling her around, putting her in a choke hold. He withdrew a knife from his front pocket and pressed it against her throat.

"Paul!" Pen shouted. "What the hell do you think you're doing? Let her go!"

"Pen, stay out of this please," Seth said, trying to keep her out of harm's way. He looked at Paul, who was slowly backing toward the water, Lucy in tow. His men fanned out around Paul, cutting off all lines of escape—on land, at any rate. Paul was making for the boat.

Shit.

"Paul, be reasonable," Seth said. "You know this isn't going to end well."

"That's right. It's going to end with this one dead." He tightened his hold on Lucy and she gasped. "This little tramp hurt Patrice," he said. "*My* Patrice. She can't trust me because of her," he said, obviously completely irrational.

"She can't trust you because her ex-husband was unfaithful," Seth told him. "He made the decision to betray Patrice, not Lucy."

"It's her fault!" he insisted, his eyes wild.

Huck, Tanner and Will moved closer, and Seth gained ground as well, but Paul continued to move toward the boat.

"Stay back," he said. "I'll cut her. You know I will."

Lucy's eyes were wide with fear.

Unfortunately, Seth was pretty sure Paul was capable of doing just that, so he didn't dare rush him the way he normally would have.

From the corner of his eye, Seth saw Trent move in behind a tree and he caught a glimpse of something in his hand. He had to flatten his lips to keep from smiling.

Brilliant.

He knew Trent wasn't going to be in a good position…but Seth was. And Trent knew that, too. He wasn't a star quarterback for nothing.

"Paul, put the knife down," Seth said again. "Let her go. You don't want to do this, man. You don't want to hurt her."

"Patrice is gone," he said. "You made her leave. Everything is ruined."

Evidently picking up on Trent's plan, Will got in on the action. "Paul, you didn't strike me as stupid and this is stupid."

"Shut up," Paul told him. "What do you know?"

"Hey, Paul," Tanner called loudly.

When the man turned his head, Trent drew back and threw the football to Seth. Then Seth quickly turned and drilled Paul right in the side of the head with it. Paul immediately dropped the knife and his hands darted to his face. Meanwhile the four of them had rushed forward and Lucy had taken advantage of Paul's pain to get away from him.

A collective cheer went through the crowd when Ranger Security had Paul safely in hand.

"Get him out of here," Trent said, immediately going to Nella and his sister.

Seth nodded.

Tanner said grimly, "I'll do the honors."

Penelope hurried forward, a look of utter horror on her face. "I can't believe… I just don't know— *Paul?*"

"Patrice was the one who introduced me to him," Monica said. "He'd been looking for a job and we'd just lost Andrew to college. I never dreamed that… They set this up from the start," she murmured. "They've been planning this for almost a year."

It boggled the mind. But then, people could be crazy and Paul was definitely off his rocker.

"Are you all right?" Seth asked, slipping a finger down Pen's cheek. She was still somewhat in shock, her skin pale beneath her light tan.

She nodded and when she looked up at him, he saw gratitude and admiration. "You were great," she said. "Nailing him with the football was a nice touch."

He merely shrugged. "Hey, I'm no Trent McWilliams, but I've spent a little time playing with the pigskin."

"And Trent knew?"

He nodded. "I'd mentioned it in passing and he knew I had a better vantage point."

"What tipped you off? What outed him?"

"The cigarette smoke. It smells like vanilla. I remembered seeing and, more importantly, smelling them in Patrice's car.

She nodded, her lips forming a soft smile. "Well done." She looked up at him. "Is everything okay now? No more surprises?"

Despite the fact that they no longer had to pretend, Seth drew her close and hugged her. No doubt she was second-guessing her instincts. After all, she'd worked with Paul for almost a year and had trusted him. "No more bad surprises," he said.

She leaned back and looked up at him. "That sounds promising."

"Good. Because it is."

"Pen, I'm so sorry," Monica repeated for the hundredth time. "I didn't know. He just seemed like a good guy. I never dreamed—"

"Mon, stop it. I didn't know either." Which was actually quite terrifying when it came right down to it. She'd trusted Paul, had even counted him as sort of a friend. He'd been to her house, he'd been entrusted with deposits for the bank. She'd never once looked at him and thought, *Wow, he might be crazy.*

When Paul had come racing around that corner and dragged Lucy with him, Pen's heart had practically landed in her throat. She'd been afraid for Lucy, but more telling, she'd been afraid for Seth, because she knew Seth was going to have to risk his life to take Paul down.

While she was certain that he was competent and she'd never doubted him, the terror that had sent her heart rate toward stroke level was wholly unexpected... and even more telling.

He was supposed to be her pretend boyfriend, completely fabricated and fake, and yet nothing had ever felt further from counterfeit in her life.

And the genuineness of the feelings she was experiencing as a result of this revelation scared the hell out of her.

12

CONFIDENT NOW that everything had been done to the best of his ability, Seth hung back and simply watched Penelope do her job. She was a maestro, he thought, continually amazed at how smoothly everything went. She'd changed clothes for the rehearsal and had swept her hair up into a messy updo that somehow managed to look both effortless and chic. She'd donned a silver sheath dress that moved like liquid over her curves and a pair of strappy silver rhinestone sandals. Gray pearls dangled from her ears and her eye makeup had been applied with a heavier hand, giving her a smoky look.

In short, she looked hot as hell.

And he'd willingly, gladly and hastily throw himself into the fire after her.

Strictly speaking, he knew that sleeping with her in the car today was probably not what Ranger Security had in mind when they'd suggested he pretend to be her boyfriend. Because he worked with other security agents who didn't miss a trick or a half-zipped zipper, as it turned out, he thought with remembered embarrassment, they'd known exactly what had happened. Thankfully, they'd had a pretty blasé attitude about it.

In fact, it seemed like they'd almost expected it, which should have alarmed him, particularly when he'd learned that each and every one of them had met their wives while working for the company.

Evidently he'd either lost his mind or lost the ability to care. Penelope was an amazing girl, very different, very exotic, very intriguing and so sexy she made him habitually hard. He wasn't a bad-looking guy, if he did say so himself, and the chemistry between them had been phenomenal. Beyond anything in his experience. He'd like to think—no, he knew actually—that if they'd met under different circumstances, they would have hooked up. They would be taking the same path they were on right now.

The one that would ultimately end tomorrow, he thought suddenly, a prickle of dread nudging his belly.

Or in three months, whichever came first.

The nudge turned into a kick.

Would she have kicked him to the curb? Seth wondered. Would she have really bailed on a relationship with him? Especially if things had continued to develop between them as well as they already had? Would he have cared?

Much as he was loath to admit it, he cared now. And it was more than pride talking. He liked her, dammit. She was funny and witty and gorgeous and intriguing… special.

Though she hadn't said a word—in fact, she *still* hadn't told him why she'd instigated a three-month rule—he suspected that she'd had to be the strong one in her family, the one who made things right when everything else went wrong.

When his father had walked out, Seth had felt the same way. He'd only been five, but the sensation had been there all the same. And it had only worsened the older he'd gotten. To be fair to his mother, she'd never put any sort of pressure on him to be the leader of their family. She'd done that herself, though during her illness she had certainly looked more to him than his sister. But that had been because he was the older child, not because he'd been a man. Furthermore, he knew she would have made the same request of his sister had she been the one in the military, their positions been reversed. She wanted them to be there for each other, wanted Mitchell to have Seth in his life and vice versa.

And, as much as it pained him to admit it…she'd been right.

Had he ever wanted to come out of the military? No. Had he planned on making a career out of it? Yes.

And then he would have missed everything.

He'd have missed Pen.

And somehow, that seemed like a terrible tragedy to him. His gaze slid to her again, where she was busy making sure everyone was standing where they were supposed to be and he smiled, unable to help himself. She was remarkable, his pretend girlfriend.

He could smell the scent of steaks on the grill, the spicy crab boil going on in the caterer's pots and the evening breeze as it drifted warmly over his skin. Rather than go off-site for the after-rehearsal dinner, Trent and

Nella had arranged for a meal here instead. Because the actual wedding party was small, and even smaller now that Patrice had left, it had been simple enough to arrange.

"All right," Pen finally called, clapping her hands together. "That's a wrap, people." She walked over to Nella and gave her a bracing squeeze. Though Seth couldn't hear what she was saying to her friend from here, he saw Nella smile and knew that whatever it was had been the right thing.

Trent cleared his throat. "The wedding planner says we can eat!" he called, then gave a little fist pump. Trent's gaze caught Seth's and he gestured to a plate, giving him the universal ya'll-help-yourselves gesture.

Excellent, Seth thought. Pen was a good cook, but he'd be lying if he said he wouldn't rather have a steak, particularly since he'd been smelling the meat on the grill for the past hour. He gestured to the others, then fell into line behind Pen's crew, who'd also been invited.

Because Monica had been giving him the I-know-what-you-did eye, even though he was certain she didn't, Seth decided to rib her a little.

"You know what your ring tone is on Pen's phone?" he asked.

"Sure. It's Randy Newman's 'You've Got A Friend In Me.' From *Toy Story*, remember?"

"Nope."

She looked up at him. "Nope you don't remember or nope that's not right?"

"Nope, that's not right." He looked ahead. "It's the theme song to *Jaws*."

She gasped, her eyes narrowed and then she whirled around. "That's all right," she finally said. "Mine for her is 'Beast of Burden.'"

Seth guffawed, which naturally drew Pen's attention. Evidently suspecting something was amiss, she walked over. "What's so funny?" she asked suspiciously.

"Nothing," he lied.

"*Jaws,* Penelope? Seriously?"

Pen gasped and glared up at Seth, then whacked him on the arm. "Snitch," she hissed.

"She says yours is 'Beast of Burden,'" he remarked mildly, then waited for the fallout.

To his surprise, Monica turned around and whacked him, too. He laughed even harder.

"He might be good-looking," Monica said to Pen, "but looks aren't everything."

"Er…I'm standing right here."

"I know," Monica drawled. "I'm freezing in your shadow, Sasquatch."

Pen snickered and shot Monica a look of admiration. "That was good."

"Thanks," she said, displaying what he imagined was a rare bit of modesty.

"Right here," he reminded them again.

Monica shivered dramatically and hurried forward, leaving them to themselves.

"You all right?" he asked, inspecting her face for traces of residual stress.

"I will be, once it all goes off without a hitch," she said, allowing the server to fill her plate with shrimp, sausage and potatoes.

They each got a drink, then Seth jerked his head toward the pier. "Wanna go down there and sit on the dock?" he asked.

She hesitated and he knew she was thinking about her crew.

"I'm still your pretend boyfriend, you know," he told her, smiling down at her.

At least until tomorrow night, anyway, Seth thought.

"Sure," she said and, without prompting, put her hand in his.

He grinned.

"OUR FEET AREN'T shark bait here, are they?" Pen asked, dangling her bare toes into the water.

Seth chuckled, the sound intimate and easy. "I don't think so." He popped a bite of shrimp into his mouth and made a sound of pleasure. "This is excellent."

"It doesn't get any better than fresh," she said. She really should have avoided the corn on the cob, Pen thought, because it invariably got stuck in her teeth and she ended up with butter running down her chin. But it smelled too good to resist. She looked over at him.

"I'm going to eat this corn," she warned him. If she was less attractive as a result of it, he'd just have to get over it.

He blinked, evidently baffled. "Okay. Are you allergic or something? Is there a reason I need to know this?"

"None, other than the fact that it's probably going to get stuck in my teeth and drip down my chin." And wouldn't that be sexy?

Another chuckle, this one louder, rumbled from deep in his chest. He gestured to the corn on his own plate. "Is it going to disgust you if I eat mine?"

"Not at all. I just thought I should give you fair warning. And by all means, please tell me if it does get stuck in my teeth. Don't let me sit here looking like a moron when you can help me out."

"Do I strike you as the kind of man who would let you look a moron?"

She chewed the inside of her cheek. "Not particularly."

He grunted and took a deliberate bite of his own corn. "Good."

She laughed, then helped herself as well and they ate in companionable silence for a while. Trent and Nella's favorite country music song drifted down to them along with the sound of laughter and happy people. This was what a wedding was supposed to be about, Pen thought. This was the reason she did what she did. She worked hard to create the perfect atmosphere, the perfect backdrop for her couple's nuptials and nothing made her prouder than when they drove away, thrilled with the promise of a new beginning together and completely blissed out over the sheer magnificence of their wedding.

"How's Nella?" Seth asked. "I haven't had a chance to talk to Trent since he told her everything."

"She's hurt," Pen told him. "She knew that Patrice had turned against marriage after her divorce, but she hadn't realized that the craziness of her hatred had poisoned her so much that she'd destroy Nella's wedding gown."

Honestly, there was a part of Pen that thought that, secretly, Patrice had known that Trent would never betray Nella the way that Alex had betrayed her. Pen was certain that Patrice resented Nella for her happiness, happiness that Patrice thought should have been hers.

"And Lucy?"

Pen took a sip of her wine, enjoying the warmth of the alcohol moving through her. "You know, Nella's actually relieved to know the truth. She said that she and Lucy had always gotten along fine until she and Trent had become engaged. Then Lucy had basically turned on her."

"Because Patrice turned on her, right?"

"Exactly. She said she just liked knowing that, ultimately, they were going to be okay."

"I noticed that she's still in the wedding party," Seth remarked. He wiped his mouth with a napkin and carved off a bit of steak.

"Yes," she said. "Because they are going to be sisters."

"And you simply eliminated one of the groomsmen?"

"Yes," Pen said. "It was the simplest solution. Trent promised his friend Tuck that he could still wear the tux so that the girls would be into him."

Seth's laugh echoed over the water and he shook his head. "Why do I get the impression this is not the strangest thing you've ever heard?"

"Because it's not. Those groomsmen always score big with the women. Haven't you ever been to a wedding?"

"Only one," he said. "My sister's. And we know how that turned out."

She winced. "I'm sorry," she said. "Have you talked to her again?"

"I checked in a little while ago. She's fine," he said. "Or as fine as she can be when she doubts every decision she makes."

"It happens, unfortunately," Pen said. "But she'll find someone better next time." She grinned and rolled her eyes. "Honestly, if she comes from your gene pool, then she's got to be beautiful."

He turned to look at her, his grin endearingly crooked, those dark green eyes twinkling with satisfaction and humor. "She is, thanks."

"Does she have green eyes, too?"

He nodded and though he didn't do anything to indicate something had shifted, she felt a wall go up all the same. "We both do."

She was treading into dangerous territory, she knew, but couldn't stop herself. "And is this a trait you inherited from your mother or your father?"

"My mother," he said, looking away. "With luck, we didn't inherit anything at all from our father."

Pay dirt. "That bad, was he?"

"Good? Bad?" He shrugged. "I wouldn't know. He didn't hang around long enough for me to form an opinion. He split when I was five and by the time I found out what a faithless bastard he was, I was old enough to kick his ass."

She tried not to betray the shock she felt and busied herself with another sip of wine. "Did you?"

"Not until he called my mother a nagging bitch," Seth said quite matter-of-factly, as though it was nothing. "Then I pummeled the hell out of him."

She'd just bet he did. And who could blame him? She certainly didn't. "I'm sorry, Seth," she said, laying a hand on his arm.

"Don't be," he told her. "I'm not."

"Did your mother ever remarry?"

He shook his head and something about the question made him smile. "No. She had a 'friend'—" he slid her a look "—but she said she'd had all of marriage she wanted and she'd leave it to the young and the stupid."

Penelope felt her eyes widen and a laugh bubble up in her throat. "She sounds like a really interesting woman," she said, and meant it.

Seth sighed, a smile still on his lips, but it had turned sad. "She was," he said softly.

Was? Oh, hell.

"Cancer is a miserable bitch of a disease," he muttered, tossing back the rest of his wine.

"Yes, it is. How long ago?"

"Seven months. And there's not a day that goes by that I don't miss her, that I don't expect a phone call, that I don't think about her," he confessed.

Because he was essentially orphaned or because he'd loved her that much? Somehow she knew it was the latter. And, though he hadn't admitted it, she also instinctively knew that his mother was the person to whom he'd kept his promise.

That's why he'd come out of the military.

Because his sister and nephew were alone and their country was fighting wars in two different countries. His mother must have been terrified that he wouldn't come back, that his sister and little Mitch would lose the only person they had left. So she'd asked him to come home.

And he'd done it.

Her eyes watered.

He'd promised to give up his career…and he had. She swallowed, moved and awed.

"She must have been something else to earn that kind of regard," Pen finally said.

"She was," he confirmed, giving her a smile. He nudged her shoulder. "She would have liked you."

"No doubt I would have liked her as well." She cleared her throat, tucked a loose strand of hair behind her ear. "How are your sister and Mitch coping?"

He kicked a bit at the water around his feet. "Like me, Katie has her good days and bad days, but the good days are getting more and more frequent," he said. "Mitch asks for Mom every once in a while, but not nearly as often as he did in the beginning. It's not that I think he's forgotten her—he still points to her picture and says her name—but he's getting used to her not being around." He grimaced. "And to me, that's actually worse."

She winced and laid a hand on his thigh. "I'm sorry, Seth. My mother and father both drive me crazy, but they're still around. I can't imagine a world without them in it, even though I know it's one I'll have to face someday."

He wiped a bit of butter off her chin and, though she should have been embarrassed, she wasn't. In fact, she found it strangely romantic. "You've probably worked it out for yourself," he said. "But Mom's the one I made the promise to. When we knew she wasn't going to get better."

"I thought you said you lost a bet."

He laughed. "I did. To her. We played poker for it."

She blinked at him, certain she'd misunderstood. "Poker? Seriously?"

He nodded. "She taught me. She was a helluva player, too."

She studied him with new appreciation. "Did you let her win?"

"I would have, but I didn't have to. She'd have won anyway. Four of a kind, aces high with a one-eyed jack."

"A wild card."

"Not just any wild card, *my* wild card, the one that invariably winds up in my hand," he told her. He slid his sleeve up and showed her a tattoo on his left shoulder. It was a perfect replica of a jack of hearts.

She smiled and shook her head. "I really hate that I never got to meet your mother."

"I do, too," he said, studying her thoughtfully.

"Would she have cheated?" Pen asked.

"At that point, possibly, but I don't think she did." He shrugged. "She knew I'd do whatever she asked. Playing the game was just for old time's sake."

Pen was quiet for a moment. "You're a good son."

He looked back out over the water again. "She was a good mother."

IF SHE THOUGHT he was going to bare his soul and expect nothing in return, then she'd better think again, Seth thought as he watched Penelope out of the corner of his eye. She knew it, too, Seth thought. She hadn't moved a muscle or even batted a lash, but he felt her tense up all the same. It was bizarre being this tuned into someone, this aware of her every mood, but he couldn't say that he didn't like it.

In fact, there were times when it came in handy. Like when they were in the backseat of a borrowed SUV.

She smiled and shook her head. "You're just going to wait me out, aren't you?"

He blinked innocently. "I don't know what you mean."

"Liar."

She heaved an exasperated, resigned sigh. "Go ahead and ask whatever you want to ask," she said. "And I will try to answer as honestly as possible."

"What's your favorite flavor of ice cream?" he asked, just to throw her off.

She frowned. "Didn't I include that in the file?"

He chuckled. "It was one of the few things you left out."

She glared at him, but her lips fought back a smile. "You're never going to let me live that down, are you? I told you I liked to be thorough," she said, drying her fingers with a napkin. "Some of this stuff could come up. We still have tomorrow to get through," she reminded him. "When someone asks you how I like my pancakes—"

"With peanut butter instead of syrup," he supplied, remembering that odd little insight.

"—then you're going to be glad you know," she finished.

He shot her a wry grin. "I'm sure that's going to be one of the first things I'm asked about you. But you never answered the question I just asked."

She inclined her head. "Ah. Favorite ice cream. Definitely butter pecan. And, incidentally, my favorite holiday dessert is pecan pie."

His was, too. His mother had made two different varieties, one just a simple pie, the other with chocolate chips and hot fudge. That had always been Katie's favorite. Would she make them this year for the holidays? Seth wondered. Had his mother shared the recipes? Or had they been lost along with her?

"What's yours?" she asked.

"Favorite ice cream or favorite dessert?"

"Both."

"I thought it was my turn to ask some questions?" he groused good-naturedly.

"You'll get your chance," she said.

"You're just delaying the inevitable, you know," he told her.

She merely smiled.

Seth looked away and released a breath. "My favorite ice cream is vanilla," he said. "I know it's very boring, but it's also very good, There's a lot to be said for things that aren't complicated and are still worth having."

She inclined her head and something unreadable shifted behind her too perceptive gaze. He knew he'd just given her a little insight, but he had no idea what it was. "I agree."

"As for my favorite pie—" He shrugged. "Like you, it's pecan." He grimaced. "I've never been a big pumpkin fan."

She nodded knowingly. "Anti-pumpkin, not anti-meringue. Noted."

He searched her gaze, waiting to see if she'd volunteer the information she knew he wanted before he had to ask. "Is it really so hard to tell me?"

She smiled and shook her head, evidently resigned at last. "What do you want to know first? Why I don't ever want to get married? Why I'm the commitment-phobic wedding planner?" she joked. "Or why I won't date anyone longer than three months?"

"Considering I think the two are related, then you choose."

She braced her arms on the pier and leaned back, letting her feet dangle freely. Though she was trying to look calm and relaxed, he knew better. Her jaw was flexed tight and her spine was utterly rigid.

"My parents have nine marriages between the two of them and my mother's fourth is on the rocks."

Nine? Damn. He had already suspected some broken marriages based on the casual references she'd made to "a stepdad" or "a stepmom," but nothing on that scale.

Her lips twisted with droll humor. "I've shocked you, haven't I?"

No point in lying. "Yes," he admitted. "Yes, you have."

"There you go."

"What do you mean, there you go?"

"That's my reason. I've seen them say 'I do' *nine* times and each time, it's been a lie." She shook her head, drew her legs up and wrapped her arms around them. "I don't want that. I don't want to want it. I don't want to believe it and then have it not be true." A bark of laughter slipped between her lips, but there was no humor in the sound. "To tell you the truth, I don't think I *could* believe it. I think I'd always be waiting for the other shoe to drop, for the man I chose to make his exit scene."

Seth took a moment to absorb her words. "So you're saying you don't think you're a better judge of character than either one of your parents?"

"I'm saying that it doesn't matter how good a judge of character you are, people can change. Love makes you stupid." She grinned at him. "I'm in your mother's camp on that one. I don't want to be stupid. I want to date and enjoy that first thrill of a new romance, then move on before it gets all complicated. Before any expectations are made."

His eyes widened and he laughed, then shook his head. "Oh, man, if I didn't have carnal knowledge of you, I'd think you were a guy."

She grinned. "Nope. I'm just a girl with a guy's commitment to self-preservation."

That was one way of looking at it, he supposed. Honestly, he didn't know what he'd truly expected her to say when he'd forced her to have this conversation. But now that he'd had it with her, he felt a bit…used.

Which was ridiculous considering that he'd gone into the relationship with no intention of taking it to the next level, of letting this be anything more than a casual, mutually satisfying fling. He'd had the same intentions she'd had and yet now that she'd admitted hers, he felt differently?

What the hell was wrong with him?

Come tomorrow, they were going to go their separate ways. She'd head back to Marietta and continue with her busy wedding season and he'd go back to Atlanta and Ranger Security would send him on to his next job. But he was going to make damned sure it didn't involve another woman. And it damned sure wouldn't require him to sign on as another pretend boyfriend.

Because at some point over the weekend, he'd stopped pretending. He'd started thinking about seeing her beyond the weekend.

But clearly not past three months.

And he had entirely too much pride to follow her along for the next ninety days, then let her kick his ass to the curb when their expiration date hit.

"I shouldn't have told you," Pen said, studying him thoughtfully.

"Why?" Better that she had, really.

She slid a finger along his jaw. "Because you look like you wished I hadn't."

He did, but he'd asked. "Nah," he said. "I just think it's a little sad, that's all."

"How so?"

He made himself grin. "Always the wedding planner, never the bride," he improvised.

She nodded once. "I'm good with that."

He sincerely doubted it, but he wasn't going to argue with her. She didn't want to risk getting hurt, not because she was afraid of the outcome, but because she was afraid it wouldn't be worth it, because she was afraid of being wrong.

And, truthfully, in her shoes, he'd probably feel the same way. Hell, he'd decided to remain single for less reason than that. He'd just never liked the odds.

Of course, he'd never met anyone who made him want to defy them—until now.

The irony wasn't lost on him and he chuckled softly.

"What's funny?"

"Us," he said, shooting her a look. "We've got less than a dozen good hours left in this bogus relationship of ours and instead of spending them in bed like proper hedonists, we're out here on the pier baring our souls."

She leaned over and kissed him, just the sweetest caress against his lips. "I've rather liked it."

He nodded. "I have, too," he admitted.

She shook her head. "You sound surprised."

"That's because I am." He slid a thumb over the soft slope of her cheek. "But you're easy to talk to."

"And there were things you wanted to know in return," she added knowingly.

He grinned and nodded without hesitation. "There is that."

"There was more than one condom in your wallet, right?" she asked, her lids dropping to half-mast. Her voice had taken on that husky quality that he loved, the low-pitched tones that called to his penis like a snake charmer. Not the best analogy, he imagined, but definitely the most accurate.

"No, but there's an entire box in the cabinet beneath the sink in my bathroom."

"Did an inventory, did you?"

He stood and pulled her to her feet, then slung an arm over her shoulder. "You're not the only one who likes to be thorough."

13

HE WAS RIGHT, PEN thought as she and Seth made their way back to the guesthouse. They did only have a few hours left to make the most of being together. And though sitting outside and talking to him had been more wonderful and cathartic than she'd ever imagined—hell, she'd told him more than she'd ever told any of her closest friends—there were definitely better ways they could be spending their time.

The second he closed the door behind them, she fastened her arms around his neck, then leaped up and wrapped her legs around his waist. He kissed her again, the same slow, thorough excavation of her mouth that he'd done before, but there was an urgency in his touch, a need to possess that she not only understood but felt as well.

He growled low in his throat, a masculine purr that reverberated deep in her womb. Then he promptly carried her into his bedroom, momentarily bypassing the bed to get the condoms. He carefully laid her down and followed her onto the mattress. She leaned up so that he could unzip her dress, then quickly dragged it out of the way. To her vast relief, he finally removed his shirt and she was able to feast her eyes on the beautiful perfection of his chest. Tawny hairs dusted his skin in whorls of gold and then formed a thin line which disappeared below his shorts. She was suddenly hit with the urge lick that line, to see if it tasted as delicious as it looked.

And then she decided that she would.

She rolled him onto his back and started at a flat crown of a nipple, then on to the middle of his chest and lower. He chuckled darkly and made quick work of releasing the back clasp of her bra. Her breasts slid free and he tossed the bra aside and palmed her, his big hands feeling wonderful against her aching flesh. He thumbed a nipple and she gasped, then slipped the button lose from its closure on his shorts.

He sucked in a harsh breath when she took him in hand and began to slide her palm over the slippery skin, working him gently. *Hers, all hers, at least for tonight,* Pen thought. Before she could consider any further depraved things she could do to him, he pulled her up, rolled her over and settled between her legs.

He was hot and heavy and hard and she instantly arched up, licking a path up his throat. He reciprocated in kind, tasting the skin between her breasts before slowly circling each globe with his mouth, building the anticipation of when he'd finally take her nipple. He did and she moaned, pushing her hands into his hair and over his wonderful shoulders and sleek, muscled back. He was utterly gorgeous, a work of art, a masterpiece built for her pleasure.

"Another thong," he breathed, slipping a hand down her belly, into the moist curls between her legs.

"It's the only kind of panties I have," she said as his fingers parted her and stroked. She inhaled sharply. "No p-panty lines," she explained.

"I like them," he told her. "They're indecent. And sexy."

Right now, though, they were in the way. She wished he'd take them off her so that he could replace those fingers with something a little more substantial. She arched against him, silently begging him for more.

He slipped a finger deep inside and then used this thumb to massage her clit. Pleasure raced through her and her muscle clenched around him, a silent plea for more, more, please God, more.

She reached blindly over to the nightstand and fumbled with the box of condoms, almost sending the entire package to the floor. She swore and he laughed.

"Impatient, are we?"

"I want you inside me," she said. "I want to feel you above me. Your strength and your weight. I want to kiss your shoulders and lick your neck and when you're as far into me as you can go, I want to grab your ass and make you go farther," she said, her voice getting louder, stronger and more agitated with every second that passed and he wasn't between her legs, rocking above her.

He stilled and looked at her, his eyes dark and heavy lidded. "Will you not take me seriously if I say that I love you?"

She chuckled. "Get a damned condom on, Seth, or I'm going to totally believe you."

Five seconds later he was fully protected and nudging her entrance. She sighed happily, tilted her hips and beckoned him inside. He pushed slowly, determinedly, with mind-numbing, back-clawing, breath-stealing precision. And when he was fully seated inside of her, she released the breath she'd been holding.

Ah, Pen thought. *That was better.*

She looked up and her gaze tangled with his. She read something there that she knew she wasn't supposed to see, something that she wasn't altogether sure she wanted to see. Then he blinked and the moment passed as he bent forward and kissed her again, threading his hands through hers.

Pen met his kiss, sucked his tongue into her mouth and rocked beneath him. It was slow and thorough, brilliant and perfect and if he made love to her all night like this, it wouldn't be long enough.

He pumped into her, the long hard length of him hitting the sweet spot with every determined thrust. She could feel the tension building in her womb, could feel the orgasm slowly circling in on itself, getting closer and closer. She drew her legs back and anchored them on either side of his hips and rocked beneath him. He sprinkled kisses along her jawline, slid his tongue down her throat and then back up again to her ear. His hot breath fanned against her.

"Come for me, baby," he said, his voice throaty and raw with need.

She thrashed beneath him, rocked harder and felt the

clenching in her belly hit a fever pitch. He bent his head and took her breast into his mouth, giving it a long tug. Something about that determined drag made the taut line between her sex and nipple snap and she came so hard her vision went from color to black and white, then back to color, and the sound that escaped her mouth was like nothing she'd ever heard before—part keening cry, part scream. And the symphony happening in her sex was something she knew would never be repeated, music that couldn't possibly make an encore performance.

Before she could savor, commit the moment to memory, Seth promptly rolled her onto her belly, grabbed her hips and held her up, then pushed into her from behind. He pounded hard, angled deep, and her knees wobbled he felt so good.

"Seth, I— Please, I—"

He reached around her and fingered her clit, stroked it in time to his thrusts. Then his thumb pressed against the rosebud of her bottom and that slightest pressure, the barest hint of sensation, was all it took to send her hurtling over the edge again. She screamed this time, but no sound emerged. Her throat was raw. His tautened balls slapped against her weeping flesh as he pistoned in and out of her, harder and harder and faster still. He showed her no mercy, gave her no quarter and she didn't want it—she only wanted him.

It was the basest, purest, most moving sex she'd ever had in her entire life and she knew that when she left here tomorrow, she'd never be the same. He'd done something to her, Pen realized. She didn't know what, but she felt the shift all the same.

He'd ruined her, Pen thought. But if this was her downfall, then she'd gladly pay the price.

SETH DIDN'T KNOW what had come over him. One minute he'd been content to simply make love to her, to take his time and make the most of it…but then the meaning of making the most of it changed and he couldn't get his mouth on her enough, couldn't touch her enough, couldn't get into her enough. He'd gone from simply wanting to take her to making her his in every sense of the word, to making her want to rethink their pretend status and consider giving him more than a ninety-day trial period.

And then he'd decided that she was literally driving him crazy, because he was an idiot to think those things, to even consider that he could be the one to change her mind. He wished he could say he just wanted the challenge of being the only exception to her rule, but he knew better. He knew in his heart what his mind didn't want to accept. She was special.

She utterly did it for him, in every sense of the word. He wanted to listen to her talk and laugh, he wanted to learn everything about her, the things that mattered and the things that didn't. He wanted to look at the world the way she saw it and notice what the differences were. He wanted to watch her wake up in the morning when the first light of dawn touched her face and those amazing eyes fluttered open, and he wanted to spoon her in bed every night before they fell asleep. He wanted to hold her hand and kiss her fingers and walk the world with her.

In the military, he'd been lucky enough to do a bit of traveling. He'd love to walk the Great Wall of China with her, show her the headwaters of the Nile, paddle through Alaska's Inside Passage and tromp through ruined castles in Scotland. He wanted to hold her hand on the streets of New York and put his arm around her as they stared out over the Grand Canyon. Did she want to do any of these things?

He had no freaking idea. And he was rapidly running out of time to find out.

It was that time or the lack thereof that made him crazy, that made him flip her over onto her belly, then take her hard from behind. He drove into her, pounding harder and harder, her sweet rump the perfect cradle for his sex. *Narrow waist, womanly hips, the sleek swell of her bottom.*

He growled low in his throat and pushed harder, her breasts bouncing on her chest, absorbing his frantic, desperate thrusts.

Another keening cry ripped from her throat and he knew that she was close again. He reached around her and stroked her clit and he felt her tighten around him again.

"Do it again," he told her.

"Seth, dammit. I—"

He smiled as she tightened again, fisted harder around him. He pushed and pulled, stroked and played, then bent forward and nipped playfully where her neck met her shoulder.

She shattered around him once more.

Seth smiled with victory and then raced toward his

own release. The sensation built and built and then, to his astonishment, she reached back and stroked his tightened balls. That one touch sent him into oblivion. Light faded, sound receded, a long growl broke loose from his throat and he shuddered behind her, emptying his seed into the end of the condom.

Breathing heavily, he carefully withdrew, disposed of the protection, then followed her down onto the bed, dragging her to him so that he could feel her against his side. She cuddled in, slinging a leg over his, an arm around his waist, her head resting on his still racing heart.

"Wow," she said, her lips pressing against his chest in a reverent kiss. "That was—"

"Beyond description," he supplied when she couldn't finish.

She nodded, her silky hair tickling his side. "That too," she said.

"Too?"

"I was going to say 'freaking awesome' but your description is more poetic."

He chuckled, tracing circles on her upper arm. He wanted to do more of this, too, Seth thought. He'd never expected to enjoy pillow talk, but imagined it would depend on whether you liked the person you were sharing the pillow with.

"I don't believe I've ever been accused of being poetic," he said, laughing.

"Bet you've been accused of being a lot of other things though, haven't you?" she teased.

"Most recently I was accused of being a smart-ass,

but that was by a mouthy little commitment-phobic wedding planner, so I didn't listen."

She playfully punched him on the chest. "You should," she quipped. "She sounds like a remarkable woman."

"She is," he admitted. "But she's awfully full of herself."

"What?" she gasped, whacking him again.

"How many more times are you going to hit me?" Seth asked. "Am I going to have file domestic abuse charges against you?"

She snorted. "I dare you. A big guy like you filing charges against a little thing like me? They'd laugh you out of the police station."

"Huck was right," Seth muttered, looking thoughtfully at the ceiling in the darkness. "Women are diabolical."

"Ha," she harrumphed. "Only out of necessity," she said. "If men weren't such know-it-alls, women wouldn't have to be diabolical."

He laughed. "I didn't say I didn't like it."

She stilled and a little gasp slipped through her lips. "You think it's sexy, don't you?"

"When it's the right woman," he said, pressing a kiss to the top of her head.

"You probably find it so attractive because you recognize it in yourself," she told him. "Like is attuned to like."

"Do you think we're alike?" he asked. For whatever reason, her answer was more important than it should have been.

She hummed under her breath for a moment, truly considering the question before answering. "Yes," she finally admitted. "I do think we're a lot alike. We both come from broken families, mine more shattered than yours in some ways, and we're both very purpose-driven. You need to have something to do, the same desire to be useful as I have, if not more," she said, displaying a keen bit of insight. "And we're both determined to meet the world on our own terms." She sighed. "And we both keep our promises. You kept yours to your mother and I keep mine to my clients. Being truthful is important, a lost art, even, and it takes courage to be honest when it would be easier to bow to diplomacy." He felt her grimace. "I would have made a piss-poor diplomat."

He laughed and hugged her tighter. "Oh, I don't know about that. You handle your team and your clients with a certain amount of diplomacy. For instance, when Nella's mother arrived with that god-awful blue rhinestone-encrusted hat she intended to wear tomorrow, you told her that the rhinestones would cast little blue glares all around the tent, possibly even against Nella's dress, making it look stained. That was pretty damned diplomatic."

She'd begun to chuckle halfway through his comment and was now struggling to stop. "Oh, jeez, did you see that thing? What the hell was she thinking? It looked like something The Little Mermaid would wear. It was ghastly." Her laughter finally tittered off. "Okay, I suppose I'm better at diplomacy than I thought I was."

He knew it, Seth thought, and fully imagined he'd

be getting a very diplomatic kiss-off tomorrow, when their pretend relationship was over.

The thought was more depressing than he would have ever imagined. He pulled her closer, kissing her once again, and beat back melancholy with the best thing available, the only known cure. God help him…

Her.

14

AH, PEN THOUGHT, the moment she'd been waiting for, the one that made every wedding worthwhile, the minute that Trent and Nella raced through a shower of birdseed and well-wishers on their way to their new life together.

Pen hung back and watched it all unfold and, to her surprise, Nella's gaze sought hers out. Her old friend blew her a kiss and mouthed a watery thank-you. Trent sent a deferential nod in her direction and the thoughtful gesture from the famous quarterback was one she'd always appreciate. Monica slid in beside her. "Well done, boss," she said. "Disaster averted, business and jobs intact, no bloodshed, all's well that ends well."

Pen repressed the unreasonable urge to cry. Something wasn't going to end well and that was her relationship with her pretend boyfriend, the sexy man who'd somehow managed to carve a place in her heart over the past three days.

It was insane.

Great sex and a few laughs did not a relationship

make, Pen told herself. And she didn't want a relationship anyway, dammit. It's what she'd been avoiding her entire adult life. She'd made a career out of attaching people, not getting attached herself.

The minute Trent and Nella were officially gone, the guys from Ranger Security would pack up their big SUV and leave, Seth with them. He wouldn't ride back with her, she knew, because there would be no need. Furthermore, his job was done and hers was not. She had to make sure that the various rental companies quickly arrived to reclaim their things and that the house and grounds were put to rights as soon as possible, especially considering that Trent and Nella actually planned to honeymoon here.

"You're awfully quiet," Monica said, studying her thoughtfully.

"Just tired," Pen said, which was, in part, the truth.

"You look like someone stole your puppy."

She managed a weak laugh. Yeah, the person who saved it from the storm drain to start with, Pen thought.

"I'll be fine," she said.

Monica nodded toward Seth. "It's him, isn't it? You like him."

If by like, Monica meant that Pen wanted to spend every minute of every day, possibly for the rest of her stupid misbegotten life, with him, then yes, that was an accurate description.

How had this happened? Pen wondered furiously. How had she let herself care for him so much? Why did he have to be the one that mattered?

This morning they'd showered together and he'd made love to her, reverently stroking and memorizing every inch of her skin. She'd caught him looking at her with this sort of furious despair, then he'd open his mouth and close it again, never saying a word. He'd made her an omelet and gotten it perfect, too, with no runny bits or crispy edges. He'd prepared her tea the way she liked it. He'd been thoughtful and courteous and utterly easy company. And for the briefest, most terrifying moment, she'd known what it would be like to be with him all the time, to go to bed with him at night and wake up with him in the morning. It would be so easy….

Too easy to believe it was true and too much of a stretch to believe it could last.

Call her a coward, call her selfish, call her whatever you wanted, Pen just couldn't bring herself to take the risk and she didn't blame him for not asking her to. There was no room for misinterpretation between them. They'd been too honest, and now she was boxed into that truth, whether she liked it or not.

He turned to look at her and a tentative smile moved over his lips. But it wasn't the genuine one she'd become used to seeing. Her heart gave a lurch as he started toward her.

Monica moved away. "I'm going to…go do something," she finished lamely, unable to come up with a good excuse to leave.

Seth took her hand in his again, causing warmth to seep into her suddenly chilled fingers. "Looks like you can make an offer on that house you wanted," he said, giving her hand a squeeze.

Whatever she'd thought he would say, that was not it. She chuckled with relief. "Yeah, I think so."

When she'd brought everything into the living room this morning, he'd seen the real estate guide lying on top of her bag and noticed the turned-down page. He'd loved it, and even knew where it was because he'd grown up in Marietta. His sister and nephew were currently living in his mother's old house only a few blocks away. He said it suited her and as far as Pen was concerned, his opinion was the only one that mattered. She planned to call her agent on the drive home today and schedule an appointment to look at the house. She wished he could go with her but knew that was something she couldn't ask.

"Everything was wonderful," he told her. "You've given Trent and Nella a memorable start to an incredible life together. You should be proud."

"I am," she said, nodding once. "Drama notwithstanding, this was one of my favorite weddings."

If he didn't leave soon she was going to lose it, Pen thought. Her heart had begun to pound, her hands were shaking and though she had never been the weepy type, her eyes were watering dangerously.

He hesitated, looked at her, then seemed to steel himself. "Trent's security team has officially taken over, so Ranger Security is finished here."

Just as she suspected. "You've done a great job," she said, managing a mangled smile. "Not bad for your first job, huh?"

He nodded, then rubbed the back of his neck.

"It's been an experience," he said. His gaze tangled meaningfully with hers. "A good one."

"Thanks," she said, her throat getting thicker by the second.

"You've been a wonderful pretend girlfriend."

He was killing her. Another horrible laugh managed to make its way past her lips. "And you've been a kick-ass pretend boyfriend."

He stared at her for a moment longer, his gaze tracing her face, lingering on her mouth. He bent forward and pressed a kiss to her forehead. It was sweet and reverent and heartbreaking and she was falling apart on the inside. "Bye, Pen," he said, his voice rough with an unnamed emotion. Then he turned and walked away.

Pen took a deep, bracing breath, then turned abruptly and headed for the beach. She was going to need a few minutes to pull herself together.

"Pen," Monica called.

She held up her hand, silently warning her assistant off, and walked faster. By the time she reached the surf, she was hyperventilating and her sides ached from trying to hold herself together.

Shake it off, Pen, she told herself. *You can do this.* Better broken now than shattered later. Better to let him go while it was her choice, than to watch him leave or wait until he grew tired of her. How many times had she watched this with her parents? Didn't she know the inevitable outcome?

Yes, she did, she thought. This way was better.

If she said it enough, maybe she'd start to believe it.

SETH SLID into the backseat of the SUV. Will and Huck shared a look he wished he hadn't seen.

They knew.

Of course, they knew, he thought. How could they not know? How could they miss the fact that he'd fallen for the wedding planner, the woman he was supposed to pretend to be in love with. *Pretend* being the operative word there. Sheesh, Lord, he'd lost his ever-loving mind, Seth thought, resisting the urge to tear out his hair. Walking away from her had been like lopping off an appendage, abandoning a part of himself he wasn't altogether sure he was ever going to get back.

How had he allowed this to happen? How in the hell had she gone from merely orbiting through his universe to becoming his whole world in a mere three days?

You'll find your rudder...and I hope she initially mops the deck with you, his mother, evidently a prophet, had said. And that was it, he realized. She *was* his rudder, a strong force in a tiny package. Aside from the maniacal sexual urges she brought out in him, hadn't he felt more grounded, more at peace, when he was with her? Hadn't he practically opened a vein and told her more than he'd ever told another living soul? Hell, even his best friends didn't know about his dad, about how he'd decked him when he'd spoken ill of his mother. And yet he'd told her, a virtual stranger.

No, not a stranger, he realized. Because in some bizarre fashion he had no way of explaining, he *knew* her. His soul had recognized hers.

He'd been done the instant she'd shown up at his door. He'd just been too dumb to realize it.

"So?" Huck finally asked when it was evident that Seth wasn't going to share.

Seth shrugged and blew out a breath. "So…mission accomplished. We're done."

"But I thought—" Will started, but stopped when Tanner punched him.

"She's a pretty opinionated woman," Will remarked with a glare at Tanner. "Reminds me a lot of Rhiannon."

"Oh?" Seth added, just to be polite. He couldn't very well tell his coworkers to shut the fuck up like he really wanted to do. It would be a piss-poor way to repay their friendship, which they'd offered in good faith.

"Yeah. Rhi knows her own mind, but sometimes it takes her mind a little while to catch up with her other feelings."

Dammit to hell, he really didn't want to talk about *feelings*.

"Jeez, Will," Huck complained, grimacing. "We all know how attuned you are to your feelings, thanks to your wife. But if it's all the same to you, we'd like to keep ours to ourselves."

That's right, Seth remembered. Will's wife was an empath and practiced emotional intelligence. She was supposedly able to pick up on other people's emotions, read them and feel them, even.

But he was thankful to Huck all the same.

"I wasn't going to talk about my feelings, jackass," Will said, thumping Huck on the back of the head. "I was merely trying to make a point."

"And that is?" Tanner asked pointedly, with a get-to-it gesture.

"A woman who knows her own mind will ultimately make the right move." He grinned, obviously remembering something pleasant. "I know mine certainly did." Will turned to look at Seth. "Let her stew for a while," he told Seth, then nodded as though he was in possession of some knowledge Seth wasn't. "She'll come around."

Seth found himself strangely heartened by Will's assertion and gave a nod in thanks, once again grateful that Garrett had recommended him for this job. No, he wasn't doing what he'd always planned to do. But he knew he was going to be happy here. His feet were on the right path.

He only wished Pen's were there with him.

PEN KNEW she was going to be in for a miserable conversation when a determined Monica burst into her office. "I know you told me to leave you alone, but I can't."

"Monica—"

"Look, Pen, you've been mopey and bitchy for a whole week! Enough is enough. Do you want to die old and alone, with nothing but a vibrator and porn to comfort you in your old age?"

"Yes," Pen said, just to irritate her. What kind of question was that anyway?

"Pen, I can't let you screw this up. I wouldn't be a good friend if I did." She leveled her gaze at Pen and took a step forward. "Pen, you are miserable without him and you know it. You—"

"I am n—"

Monica shushed her. "You *are*," she insisted. "There's no point in denying it. The truth is written in those ugly bags beneath your eyes. You look haggard and unhappy and have developed an unsightly sallow tone to your skin."

Great, Pen thought. With a friend like Monica, who needed enemies?

"And, honestly, I think it's a bit…stupid of you to continue on this way, in this self-imposed hell of your own making, just because you're too much of a coward to take a chance."

Okay, that was enough. "I am not a coward," she said, sending her assistant a warning glance. "I am *careful*. There's a difference."

"Not in this case, there's not," Monica said, undeterred. "If you'd seen the way he looked at you, you would know that you don't have to be careful with him, sweetheart. The man adores you. He's nothing like those other easily directed—Paul had had that right and you know it—pretty boys you've dated in the past, the kind who were content with the superficial relationship you were willing to offer because you were too afraid of—"

"I'm not afraid," she repeated again. But suddenly she knew in her heart it was a lie. She *was* afraid. She was terrified that she'd let her own happiness become so invested in his that she'd lose herself—that he'd leave and take that part of her with him and she'd never get it back, never get herself back.

"You are," Monica insisted. "We all are," she added more gently. "But you don't have to be afraid with him, Pen. He loves you."

Penelope's chest constricted. "He does not," she scoffed, not daring to believe. "He doesn't know me well enough to love me." She didn't know him well enough to love him either, and yet she was relatively certain she did. It would be horrible to be in this much misery over someone she wasn't in love with, that was for sure.

"I don't agree, but if he doesn't yet, then he will." She handed Pen her purse. "Go to him, Pen. Give him a chance to be different. Because he is," she added. "Abnormal size aside, he's pretty damned spectacular."

"He's not abnormally sized," she said, her throat tight. "He's perfect."

"Exactly," Monica told her. "For you."

Making a split decision, Pen grabbed her purse and headed out of the office. She considered turning around half-a-dozen times before she finally found herself standing outside Seth's apartment door, but she knew that if she didn't give this a shot, she'd regret it for the rest of her life.

She'd been regretting it forever since she'd gotten home. And it had only worsened with every day that had gone by. She'd dreamed about him, scoured wedding pictures for a glimpse of him, played Solitaire and burst into tears when she'd seen the jack of hearts.

She took a bracing breath, then lifted her hand and

knocked. Once again she heard the pad of bare feet against the floor, but unlike the last time, she knew exactly what was waiting for her.

He blinked when he saw her. "Pen?"

He was shirtless again, damn him. Didn't he know how much she loved his chest. Low-slung shorts—that's what happened when a man had virtually no hips, she thought—and bare legs and feet. She had to cross her arms over her chest to keep from leaping into his arms, from crawling all over him like a spider monkey. A strangled laugh broke in her throat, which no doubt made her look a little crazy. Which she was.

About him.

"Is this a bad time? I should have called first, but I—"

"No, no," he assured her. "Come on in. Can I get you anything?"

"A drink would be nice," she said, a departure from the last time she'd arrived on his doorstep, uninvited. She had a feeling he wasn't going to make this easy on her and she knew she was going to need a little alcohol to get her through it.

"Sure," he said, strolling into the kitchen. "A beer okay?"

"Yes, thanks." She sat on the edge of the sofa and tried to pretend her heart wasn't about to pop out of her chest, that what she was about to say really didn't matter.

He returned and handed it to her. She took a grateful sip, then looked up at him once more. He merely stared at her, quite hungrily, which was nice. But he didn't say anything.

She'd been right. He was going to make her beg.

And it was a sad testament to her current state that she'd do it.

"How've you been?" she asked.

"Pretty damned miserable," he admitted affably. "You?"

"The same."

He nodded. "I've been having a hard time seeing the point."

She hesitated. "That's why I'm here. I've been struggling with that, too. I was kind of wondering if you'd like to stop being my pretend boyfriend—"

"I thought I had."

"—and start being my real one," she finished quietly.

He stared at her, his expression unreadable. "Your real one?"

"Yes."

"Your *real* boyfriend?" he repeated, evidently because he enjoyed torturing her.

"Mmm-hmm." She waited.

"Are you going to kick my besotted ass to the curb in three months?"

Besotted? Truly? Her heart leaped and a smile slid slowly over her lips. "That's not my intent, no," she said.

"So if we're still happy in three months, you're going to let our relationship continue to grow and develop?"

"Yes."

He passed a hand over his face to hide a smile. "You're going to do my laundry and darn my socks?"

"No," she said, biting her lip to keep from laughing. Only Seth, she thought. "I will not do those things." She didn't even do her own laundry—she dropped it off at the cleaner's. And she wouldn't know how to darn a sock if her life depended on it.

"Will you occasionally fetch me a beer and scratch my back?"

Her lips twitched. "Yes. Occasionally."

"And when is this relationship supposed to start?"

"Now, preferably."

He stood and offered her his hand. When she put hers in his, he yanked her quickly forward and wrapped his arms around her. "It took you long enough," he said. "I've been sitting here all week."

"Shirtless?"

"Yes."

"Damn," she said, wincing. "If I'd have known that, I would have been here sooner."

"I had no idea you were so shallow," he teased, kissing her. Sweet emotion bolted through her.

"And I had no idea I was such a coward. I'm sorry, Seth. I was just afraid. I—"

He shushed her. "You're not a coward. You're careful. And I happen to admire that about you." He grinned down at her. "It means that I'm ultimately going to be more special than everyone else."

He already was, Pen thought as she pressed her lips to his once more.

Epilogue

Three months later...

"YOU DID WHAT?" MONICA screamed into her ear.

Pen chuckled and squeezed Seth's hand. "We just got married in Vegas," she said. "At a drive-through wedding chapel."

Evidently Jamie had put the idea into Seth's head several months ago. When he'd popped the question this morning, he hadn't wanted to wait so he'd called the airline and booked the tickets, then called his sister and shared the news. She'd been ecstatic and had happily welcomed Pen into their family.

"Pen, I'm going to kill you," Monica said. "You can't be serious. You're a wedding planner, one of Atlanta's *premier* wedding planners! How do you think this is going to affect your reputation? You—"

"See you in a couple of weeks," Pen told her, not caring in the least. "We're honeymooning in Alaska." And when they came home, it would be to the house she'd bought in Marietta. The place where they would build their family. The very idea made her throat tighten.

She snapped the phone shut and looked at her newly minted husband. Desire slid through her, making her belly go all warm and tingly. They were going to need to stop soon and consummate this marriage, Pen thought. She couldn't wait until they got to the other side of the road, much less Sitka. "She's freaking out," she said.

Seth grinned. "You knew she would."

True. And if anyone had told her three months ago that she'd be married, or that she would have done the deed in the same way a person could buy doughnuts, she would have told them they were crazy.

Turns out she was the crazy one.

Because Pen didn't care about the wedding. She only cared about the marriage…and she knew that it was going to be as strong as it possibly could be.

Seth gave her that assurance in the little ways he loved her every day. From making sure that her car was serviced to sneaking a kiss on the back of her neck when she wasn't looking, she always felt loved. And she knew she always would.

Because he'd just promised to love her until death they did part. And she knew Seth was a man who kept his promises…

* * * * *

COMING NEXT MONTH

Available February 22, 2011

REQUEST YOUR FREE BOOKS!
2 FREE NOVELS PLUS 2 FREE GIFTS!

red-hot reads!

YES! Please send me 2 FREE Harlequin® Blaze® novels and my 2 FREE gifts (gifts are worth about $10). After receiving them, if I don't wish to receive any more books, I can return the shipping statement marked "cancel." If I don't cancel, I will receive 6 brand-new novels every month and be billed just $4.24 per book in the U.S. or $4.71 per book in Canada. That's a saving of at least 15% off the cover price. It's quite a bargain. Shipping and handling is just 50¢ per book in the U.S. and 75¢ per book in Canada.* I understand that accepting the 2 free books and gifts places me under no obligation to buy anything. I can always return a shipment and cancel at any time. Even if I never buy another book, the two free books and gifts are mine to keep forever.

151/351 HDN FC4T

Name _____ (PLEASE PRINT) _____

Address _____ Apt. #

City _____ State/Prov. _____ Zip/Postal Code

Signature (if under 18, a parent or guardian must sign)

Mail to the **Reader Service**:
IN U.S.A.: P.O. Box 1867, Buffalo, NY 14240-1867
IN CANADA: P.O. Box 609, Fort Erie, Ontario L2A 5X3

Not valid for current subscribers to Harlequin Blaze books.

Want to try two free books from another line?
Call 1-800-873-8635 or visit www.ReaderService.com.

* Terms and prices subject to change without notice. Prices do not include applicable taxes. Sales tax applicable in N.Y. Canadian residents will be charged applicable taxes. Offer not valid in Quebec. This offer is limited to one order per household. All orders subject to credit approval. Credit or debit balances in a customer's account(s) may be offset by any other outstanding balance owed by or to the customer. Please allow 4 to 6 weeks for delivery. Offer available while quantities last.

Your Privacy—The Reader Service is committed to protecting your privacy. Our Privacy Policy is available online at www.ReaderService.com or upon request from the Reader Service.

We make a portion of our mailing list available to reputable third parties that offer products we believe may interest you. If you prefer that we not exchange your name with third parties, or if you wish to clarify or modify your communication preferences, please visit us at www.ReaderService.com/consumerschoice or write to us at Reader Service Preference Service, P.O. Box 9062, Buffalo, NY 14269. Include your complete name and address.

HB11

USA TODAY *bestselling author Lynne Graham*
is back with a thrilling new trilogy
SECRETLY PREGNANT, CONVENIENTLY WED

Three heroines must marry alpha males to keep
their dreams…but Alejandro, Angelo and Cesario
are not about to be tamed!

Book 1—JEMIMA'S SECRET
Available March 2011 from Harlequin Presents®.

JEMIMA yanked open a drawer in the sideboard to find
Alfie's birth certificate. Her son was her husband's child.
It was a question of telling the truth whether she liked it or
not. She extended the certificate to Alejandro.

"This has to be nonsense," Alejandro asserted.

"Well, if you can find some other way of explaining how
I managed to give birth by that date and Alfie not be yours,
I'd like to hear it," Jemima challenged.

Alejandro glanced up, golden eyes bright as blades and
as dangerous. "All this proves is that you must still have
been pregnant when you walked out on our marriage. It
does not automatically follow that the child is mine."

"'I know it doesn't suit you to hear this news now and I
really didn't want to tell you. But I can't lie to you about it.
Someday Alfie may want to look you up and get acquainted."

"If what you have just told me is the truth, if that little
boy does prove to be mine, it was vindictive and extremely
selfish of you to leave me in ignorance!"

Jemima paled. "When I left you, I had no idea that I was
still pregnant."

"Two years is a long period of time, yet you made no
attempt to inform me that I might be a father. I will want
DNA tests to confirm your claim before I make any deci-

sion about what I want to do."

"Do as you like," she told him curtly. "*I* know who Alfie's father is and there has never been any doubt of his identity."

"I will make arrangements for the tests to be carried out and I will see you again when the result is available," Alejandro drawled with lashings of dark Spanish masculine reserve.

"I'll contact a solicitor and start the divorce," Jemima proffered in turn.

Alejandro's eyes narrowed in a piercing scrutiny that made her uncomfortable. "It would be foolish to do anything before we have that DNA result."

"I disagree," Jemima flashed back. "I should have applied for a divorce the minute I left you!"

Alejandro quirked an ebony brow. "And why didn't you?"

Jemima dealt him a fulminating glance but said nothing, merely moving past him to open her front door in a blunt invitation for him to leave.

"I'll be in touch," he delivered on the doorstep.

What is Alejandro's next move? Perhaps rekindling their marriage is the only solution! But will Jemima agree?

Find out in Lynne Graham's
exciting new romance
JEMIMA'S SECRET

Available March 2011
from Harlequin Presents®.

Copyright © 2011 by Lynne Graham

HPEXP0311

Start your Best Body today with these top 3 nutrition tips!

1. **SHOP THE PERIMETER OF THE GROCERY STORE:** The good stuff—fruits, veggies, lean proteins and dairy—always line the outer edges of the store. When you veer into the center aisles, you enter the temptation zone, where the unhealthy foods live.

2. **WATCH PORTION SIZES:** Most portion sizes in restaurants are nearly twice the size of a true serving and at home, it's easy to "clean your plate." Use these easy serving guidelines:
   - Protein: the palm of your hand
   - Grains or Fruit: a cup of your hand
   - Veggies: the palm of two open hands

3. **USE THE RAINBOW RULE FOR PRODUCE:** Your produce drawers should be filled with every color of fruits and vegetables. The greater the variety, the more vitamins and other nutrients you add to your diet.

Find these and many more helpful tips in

YOUR BEST BODY NOW
by
TOSCA RENO
WITH STACY BAKER
Bestselling Author of
THE EAT-CLEAN DIET®

Available wherever books are sold!

NTRSERIESFEB

Love Inspired.
HISTORICAL
INSPIRATIONAL HISTORICAL ROMANCE

Top author
LINDA FORD
brings readers back in time
with a new heartfelt romance

PRAIRIE *Cowboy*

Conor Russell knows
what prairie living can
do to a delicate female—
that's why he's raising
his daughter, Rachel, to
be tough. And why he
knows new schoolteacher
Miss Virnie White won't
last long. But Virnie is
staying put, and is
determined to
show Conor that
strength comes
in many forms.

Available March, wherever books are sold.

www.SteepleHill.com

**Steeple
Hill®**

LIH82860

HARLEQUIN *Presents*

USA TODAY *Bestselling Author*

Lynne Graham

is back with her most exciting trilogy yet!

SECRETLY PREGNANT CONVENIENTLY WED

Jemima, Flora and Jess aren't looking for love,
but all have babies very much in mind...and they may
just get their wish and more with the wealthiest, most
handsome and impossibly arrogant men in Europe!

Coming March 2011

JEMIMA'S SECRET

Alejandro Navarro Vasquez has long desired vengeance after
his wife, Jemima, betrayed him. When he discovers the
whereabouts of his runaway wife—and that she has a two-
year-old son—Alejandro is determined to settle the score....

FLORA'S DEFIANCE (April 2011)
JESS'S PROMISE (May 2011)

Available exclusively from Harlequin Presents.

www.eHarlequin.com

HP12975